Nobody's Hero

Rob never believed he could be anybody's hero

He believed he was nobody, or nobody special.

He was a hero; he just couldn't see it.

He needed his own hero to love him and to save him.

DEDICATION

To Ronald

A friend who pulled me out of the darkness.

For all the wild memories.

You helped me grow, to learn to trust,

to love.

To Dawn

We were both fortunate to be loved by this amazing man

But you got the best part of him, his heart.

Treasure the memories.

.

This story is based on

the life of an amazing man,

Ronald Osborne.

Just like the rest of the Wildflower Series,

it is a biographical fiction.

Where truth meets fiction.

The two women who loved him most have made this

story what it is, and because of their love for him, his

character and the emotions are accurate

to honour him.

To honour Ron,

20% of all sales will go to a local charity

supporting children and young people to have

opportunities and to grow up to be happy and

healthy.

A charity he supported.

For more information on the chosen charity

Visit the website.

www.imogenkelsie-thewildflowerseries.co.uk/nobodys-hero

A Husband

I will be forever grateful for having him in my life.

I can never fathom why God would give me someone so good only to snatch them away again. I know you are safe with Him, loved and warm, but I can't reach you there.

The extraordinary unconditional love which he showed me was unbelievable.

I was his girl. His everything.
He was my man, and my everything.
My life was empty before I met him, he made me whole, my other piece of me.
I didn't function without him.

I have never known such a wonderful caring man who was not only loved by me, but also by my family and very dear friends.
The world lost angel the day I lost him, and I will honour him always for the rest of my life.
Thank you, God, for letting me have him for over ten years.

Dawn x

A friend

Ron saved me in every way a girl can be saved.

If ever there was a definition of what a true friend is, it would have him as an example.

I was nobody, he made me somebody. He showed me love and taught me how to love.
I didn't always realise what I had; at times I took his love for granted.

I will forever be thankful for having him in my life as I know I wouldn't be here if I had not met him.

I will always love you my friend.

Donna x

I'm nobody's hero...

But for you I'd lay down my life.
As long as you are by my side everything will be alright.

I am nobody's hero but for you I'd tear down the stars from the sky.
You know I'm not afraid to fight. For you I'm not afraid to die.

Don't be afraid.

When all your faith has gone, I will pray for you
Just keep holding on, I will be there for you

I've seen the storm I've been through the rain
You've got to know that I feel your pain.

When you're on the edge, I will rescue you
When you need a friend, I'll be there for you.

If you would lean on me, dream on me, and just believe in me.

I'm nobody's hero.

~ Jon BonJovi ~

Welcome to the Wildflower Series

Throughout the series we have met and fell in love with Rob.

Robert Reagan

This book continues to tell his story,
to see life Rob's eyes.
To really get to know and understand 'Nobody's Hero'.

Will he get the happy ever after he deserves?

We first met Rob in Becoming Wildflower, and Nobody's Hero Part 1.
Both showed us a moment which changed her Imogen's life forever,
the hero who saved her, and their unique friendship which ensued.

Now we move further as we are introduced to the woman who
saved his life – Frankie.

Music features highly in the Series, so much so the novel has a soundtrack of suggested songs relative to the story.

The suggested song list can be found on the website.

www.imogenkelsie-thewildflowerseries.co.uk/interactive

Love isn't something you find, it finds you.

Frankie came into Rob's life to save him.
To become the Hero that he needed...

Prologue

December

It was the Friday before Christmas. Imogen and Marcus had returned earlier that day to visit her father. What was planned as a flying visit culminating in them staying overnight to spend black-eye Friday with Rob. They ventured out to the bars in Whitley Bay on what was a mild evening. The town was buzzing with revellers, many in Christmas jumpers out on the night which for many was the start to their Christmas holidays, with many clubbing like that night was their last night on Earth. As usual the atmosphere was like no-where else. In the bars the ambience was contagious, like a virus, but a good one. There was love in the air, everyone all hyped up and ready to have a good time. Imogen was sat upon Marcus' knee, feeling blissfully content as she watched Rob weave his way back from the bar, negotiating through the crowds like a pro, without spilling a drop, his smile wider than the golden gates.

"God I love that man" She thought as she watched him return to the table placing the drinks down.

Imogen thought how blessed she was to have two amazing men in her life, the two men she loved more than anything in the world. Her eyes scanned the bar which was filled by beautiful women...

Women oblivious to the 'catch' that walked amongst them. She thought that if the veil were to fall, they would be falling at his feet. But for that to happen he would have to see his true worth.

She thought how the only thing that would make their '3' perfect would be a 4th person, someone for him to love, but also someone who would love him how he deserved. The day their family would become complete. She sat, as though lost in a daydream. Scenarios of the adventures they would have filled her mind.

She became jolted back to reality as Rob stood in front of her waving his hand in front of her eyes.

"Hello! Anyone in there?" he laughed.

"What? Yeah man!" she replied trying to shake herself back int the present as she watched the men laugh at her.

She gave an amused sigh before downing her drink.

"Come on old men! We got a night of drinking ahead!" she exclaimed climbing off Marcus' knee, biting her lip, her eyebrows raising as her crazy smile crept across her face.

An hour into the evening Charlie joined them in the Fire station pub. A few other friends had promised to join later in the evening as they meandered their way from bar to bar down South parade.

As the night progressed everyone began to fall away or become separated in the crowded bars. Rob, Imogen, and Marcus stood on the road contemplating their next move. Imogen stood bent over, her hands resting upon her knees trying to avoid thinking about the hangover to come.

It was only 10pm, the night was still young. She thought how once she could party all night and although stubbornly wanted to prove she still had it in her she knew she couldn't go on. Rob and Marcus could see her struggling to keep her balance, and she knew she was struggling to keep it under wraps.

"I need to get her home." Marcus stated as his arm slipped under hers, linking together to provide that extra support.

"What about you?" Marcus asked, feeling guilty leaving him alone.

"I'm sure you could join us, you know Bri won't mind you using the spare room? We could watch some movies? Pizza?" Marcus continued.

"I'm staying on mate" Rob replied.

Imogen urged them both to continue without her, to put her in a taxi, that she'd be fine, not wanting to leave Rob alone.

"I'm fine!" she insisted as she tried to walk up the kerb staggering towards the bar, before reaching out to steady herself, her hand resting upon the brick wall as her stomach began to heave in a sickly way feeling as though her head was spinning like being upon a carousel, slow at first but gaining momentum.

"OK! I think I'm beat! You guys stay out, I'll get a cab, I'll see you back at dads?" They both shook their heads. Marcus looked at Rob communicating without words.

Marcus smiled before turning to Imogen.

"Come on, let's get you home lightweight" declining her request that he continued without her.

Marcus looked back at Rob.

"I'll be fine, am bound to bump into others at some point, am not ready to head home yet, the night is still young" Rob declared triumphantly.

Waving them off in a taxi he sauntered down the street. He stood outside of Havannah, the bar was bustling inside and out. He entered and began walking through the club towards the bar. He stood alone in the club scanning the crowd. In the corner stood a redhead with another girl with shocking blue hair. His eyes continued to search for faces he recognised. Against the wall near the bar stood a blonde chatting with a brunette. As the blonde turned, she caught his eye, and in that moment, it was as though his world fell apart, as though somehow, she had bewitched him.

Ordering a drink, he continued to watch her. He stopped moving, stopped breathing, it felt as though the air had been knocked out of him. Entranced by this beauty who had put a spell on him.

"Had she even noticed him?" He thought to himself.

"Gorgeous" he whispered under his breath as he watched her.

Her curves were shouting his name. She had a smile worth dying for, and even across the darkened club he could see her eyes sparkling though from the distance he couldn't tell if her eyes were brown or blue. He knew he had to go nearer; it was as though she was drawing him towards her.

Her laugh was like magic and he was awe-struck by the way she tossed her hair over her shoulder as she listened attentively. He was amazed at how open and outgoing she was. Her resounding confidence overflowing. There was only one way the night was ending, and that was them leaving together. Every glance at her was making him more anxious to know her, to talk to her. He slowly began walking in her direction trying to build up the courage to make his move. The crowds disturbed his line of sight. He moved, trying to find her again but she had disappeared; his heart sank.

He'd remembered laughing at Imogen as she tried to describe her feelings that first moment that she met Marcus, but until that moment he thought Love at first sight was just a 'fairy-tale'.

He walked to the bar, buying another drink. He could think of nothing else but her. It was as if she had bewitched his very soul.

He knew he had to find her. He necked back his drink and began searching the bar, pushing himself through the crowds with no avail.

She was gone.

He left the club, entering every bar down towards parade, in hope of finding her again. The hours past. He was almost ready to give up, losing all hope. Standing at the bar, in Hairy Lemon's, holding a pint, he caught a glimpse of her on the dance floor. He couldn't hide the smile which crept across his face when he knew he'd found her.

He looked over at her, trying to build up the courage to go and talk to her.

She turned catching his eye, she smiled an innocent smile as if silently giving him permission.

He walked up to her, his hands sweating, the chemistry was undeniable. A girl had never made him feel that way before, and doubt would ever again, this was a once in a lifetime chance that he was not going to let slip through his hands.

He spun her round, lifting her off her feet.

"You're the girl for me, I've been searching for you all night" He spoke before kissing her, taking her breath away.

Goosebumps lined his skin, not the kind that comes from the cold, but the kind that only comes when nothing else matters except the 'right here, right now'. In that moment it felt like the world had slowed to an almost stop, the rest of his world becoming an unimportant blur.

"You know you have the most amazing smile and the kindest eyes" He spoke as he took a short step back until his eyes again locked on hers, the pale blue into deep emerald.

His right hand raised up to her cheekbone before tucking her golden wisps behind her ear, slowly moving in closer. Close enough for her to feel his body through her clothes. He stood waiting, contemplating his next move, wondering if it would be too much to kiss her again.

They stood as though frozen in time, he leant in further hovering for a moment. She inhaled deeply, as his lips came closer and closer to hers. His lips delicately brushed against hers. Their breaths mingled. His arms encircled her as they kissed. Feeling the caress of her lips upon his were softer than he could ever have imagined, filled with swirls of emotion he savoured each moment.

Breaking away she stepped back smiling a sweet yet slightly seductive smile which had him entranced. Slowly she turned walking away towards the door, leaving him stood speechless unable to move as though glued to the spot.

"Well, you coming?" she spoke casually as she turned looking in his direction.

Startled, he downed his pint grabbing his jacket before hastily following her like a lost puppy who had fallen head over heels in love.

They walked down towards the promenade looking out across the shore. They spent the rest of the night and into the following morning together talking. He didn't want to see her go, worried that once she was gone, he would never see her again.

The hours past, the streets became empty as the sky began to become light from the rising sun. Dawn was breaking disturbing the darkness of the night. They began walking up into town until they stumbled upon a café which was open for business. They walked in through the white framed glass door which looked as though it was ready to fall from its hinges. They sat at a table with him still holding onto her hand, not wanting to let go. The café provided a soft dim light from the old lightbulbs which were slowly becoming enveloped by the light from outside.

They sat drinking coffee and sharing a cooked breakfast. He didn't want to leave, to be parted from her. She scribbled her number on a napkin. Ring me... she said as she exited the café.

The rest of the morning was a daze as he returned home and collapsed on to his bed trying to make sense of the night before.

That night marked a new beginning, not that he knew it. Before that night, before Frankie he thought he knew what his life was supposed to be, who he was, but after meeting her, well, there was just after...

Chapter 1

Rob sat alone in his flat. A small, crumpled piece of paper in his hand, on it was scrawled a phone number. Contemplating ringing it like he had so many times since that initial meeting. He also wondered whether the number was real or if she'd given him a fake number.

It had been almost 2 weeks since that night, a few nights before Christmas.

It was now the 30th December.

He'd spent a few hours on Christmas day with his baby girl but spent the remainder alone. Hating the loneliness, he'd decided to spend a few days in between Christmas and New Year in Scarborough with Imogen and Marcus. He had mastered being alone, as everyone else's journeys always separated from his, but that period was always the hardest; reminding him of what was missing, killing him a little bit more. Though that year there was a renewed sense that maybe his life was about to truly begin, that maybe he was being allowed to find happiness.

While there he told Imogen of that night, of that girl who had changed his world in a moment confessing that he never rang her, not wanting to ruin the perfect night.

He remembered Imogen's reaction…

"and… So, what happened next?? Did you ring her??" she asked inquisitively, distracting herself from her thoughts.

He looked away shrugging. "Nah, not yet anyways. Doubt she'd even remember me"

Imogen pushed him, hitting him across the shoulder with her strappy stiletto shoe.

"You big idiot!" What am I going to do with you?"

"Ow, that hurt, you bully!" he protested.

"Well I need to knock some sense into you. Ring her! You big goof!" she replied.

He began rubbing his shoulder remembering her hitting him with her stiletto shoe and remembering the final words she said before leaving…… Ring Her!!

He'd promised he would, but still he sat there feeling unable to do it. Rob sighed as he placed the piece of paper and his phone on the table before standing up pacing the floor.

Frankie was thinking back to that night... Was he real?

Memories of meeting him faded into a dream, the same as a dream she played time and time again. She felt good with him in a way she hadn't before or since.

It had been a normal girl's night out the Friday before Christmas. Getting ready with her friend Catrina she had no idea that night would change her life.

They spent the night going bar to bar like any other night. They were in Hairy Lemons when she spotted him.

He looked over at her.

She couldn't help but be drawn to that smile, the biggest smile she'd ever seen, she smiled back before turning to avoid his gaze.

She tried to distract herself by making conversation with Catrina, and continued sipping her drink, trying to resist the urge to look back at the tall dark and handsome man who had caught her eye.

She turned hoping to catch one more glimpse to find him standing there in front of her. It was as though he was destined to walk into her life. He'd walked up to her with a confidence, an assurance, as though he knew he was a God and she wondered if the universe had led her there on that night.

She thought, "Surely he's looking for someone other than me."

"Hi, I'm Rob" he spoke breaking her thoughts.

"Hi" she replied before diverting her gaze to everywhere but on him.

"Are you single?" he queried.

She gave a slight nod still trying to avoid looking at him though was finding it almost impossible feeling unable to avoid the connection.

Looking into those deep brown eyes the chemistry was undeniable.

In those moments it felt as though time had stood still, the loud music seemed to fade to a background noise, as though she could be able to hear a pin drop. The rest of her world becoming an unimportant blur.

There was a kind of static atmosphere between them, like magnets being drawn to each other, she wondered if he could feel it too or whether it was all one-sided.

She wondered if he was just a player and she was his latest conquest, or if it was destiny and fate taking control of chance - to give her a chance, a chance to take that leap.

He moved in closer with those eyes that look so deeply into her own,

"You're the girl for me, I've been searching for you all night" he whispered before lifting her off her feet, spinning her before kissing her, taking her breath away.

As they broke apart her breathing became softer, gazing upon his pensive look which melted into a smile as soft as the morning light. There was something about that gaze from him, a look that she had never seen before and knew she would never find in another man.

"You know you have the most amazing smile and the kindest eyes" He spoke as he took a short step back until his eyes again locked on hers.

His right hand raised up to her cheekbone before tucking her golden wisps behind her ear, slowly moving in closer. Close enough for her to feel his body through her clothes.

She stood waiting, contemplating his next move, wondering if he would kiss her again, or if she should step forward and kiss him back.

They stood as though frozen in time, he leant in further hovering for a moment. She inhaled deeply, as his lips came closer and closer to hers.

She walked through her flat wondering why he hadn't rung her and had begun to give up on any hope that he would. Her hope was fading with each passing day as she began to think he hadn't felt that same connection.

Rob stopped pacing the floor, his hands gripped the back of the dining chair staring at his phone and the piece of paper.

"Well here goes!" he spoke out loud as though to give himself encouragement to take that step.

He picked up his phone typing in the number. He stared at the number on his screen as his finger hovered above the call button. His finger pressed against his phone screen triggering the dialling tone. As the phone began to ring, he knew there was no turning back.

"Hello…"

He took a deep breath as he heard her voice.

"Who is this?" she asked.

His heart skipped a beat, the words wouldn't take form.

"Hi it's Rob…. From the other night in Whitley…. " His voice was trembling, feeling breathless and weak, a chaos within his chest, feeling as though his heart would explode from his chest hearing her voice.

"I don't know if you remember me or not…" he continued hesitantly.

They talked for what felt like forever arranging to meet up for their first official date.

The following day…

New Year's Eve.

Chapter 2

He waited for her outside of Baĉa, his focus was scattered, filled with nervous anticipation, a whirl of emotions, excited, even giddy. As he waited the snow began to fall turning the quaint little village into a magical picturesque scene. He saw her approach.

As she neared, he leant in kissing her upon the cheek though he wanted to kiss her properly like they had that first night. He took hold of her hand, their fingers entwined in a loose grip. A tingling feeling began to spread throughout his entire body as they walked down the path towards the Salutation.

They entered the bar trying to get past the nervous awkwardness.

"Would you like a drink?" he asked as he pulled out her chair.

As she sat, she took in a shallow breath before slowly exhaling. She wasn't focusing on his words but instead was absorbed in his voice. She thought how his voice was so warm and rich; her heart began to beat faster.

There was a silence as he stood behind, his hands resting on the back of her chair waiting for a response.

Frankie turned slightly, looking at him waiting for her to answer, she began to blush.

"Sorry... I'll have a gin and tonic if that's OK?" she replied.

His look of bafflement became a shy smile which melted her heart.

She watched him walk away towards the bar, admiring his figure. Though she still couldn't get that smile out of her mind. She thought how some wear a smile, but he didn't just wear it, he was the smile.

She watched as he moved through the bar, everything about him was a soft and understated joy as he greeted each person no matter who they were.

Returning with the drinks he sat opposite with heavy awkwardness, not wanting to mess up that night because never seeing her again was not something he wanted. His insecurities played on his mind asking himself what she saw in him and thinking once she got to know him and the façade became stripped away, she would be gone forever.

He sat drinking his pint in the hope that alcohol would calm him and give him the confidence he needed.

Frankie sat looking at him taking in his cheekbones, full lips and that caramel skin that she just wanted to have so close. As she continued to watch him, she thought how there was something so sexy in that vulnerable look of his, wondering what was going through his mind.

She broke the silence which also broke the dam.

Every softened word he spoke invaded her mind. She responded to his awkward attempt at humour not with derision or with faked laughter like he was used to, instead finding someone with whom interaction did not stop and jolt along fumbling social cues. That warm voice sent her emotions into overdrive, a feeling of warmth, igniting a spark, wrapping her body in a blanket of comfort while at the same time consuming her soul in the heat of lust.

She could feel herself becoming infatuated in this man that she barely knew but felt safe with. His smile continued to send her mind into an uncontrolled, captivated spiral. She couldn't help but hope that those feelings would grow into something deeper.

He became lost in her smile and her laugh was unrestrained as though taking over her whole body.

He secretly smiled realising it was all because of him. He was proud of himself, proud that he'd been the one to make her smile, to make her appear so happy.

They sat talking for hours, losing track of time. Rob stared up at the clock. 11.50pm. Only 10 minutes left of that year. He began to reflect, taking a moment to see how far he had come in just twelve months. A year of ups and downs, a year full of turmoil , the year he became a father. Reflecting on his emotional journey and the progress which he had been beginning to forge. Focusing on the relationships that really mattered.

As midnight approached and the bar resonated with a countdown, he held her hands across the table, looking deep into her eyes thinking how that year was also the year he first saw her face and fell in love for the first time in his life. Something he never believed would happen, something he never felt worthy of. He wondered whether she would be a part of his life from then on, would he be good enough? Could he be enough for her?

As the words 'Happy New Year' resounded through the bar he smiled.

"Happy New Year" he spoke quietly for only her to hear.

He leant across the table; their lips touched. As their lips parted, he looked at her and in that moment, he only allowed himself to dwell on positive thoughts, letting them soak in a little deeper, before taking a deep and relaxing breath.

He smiled.

"The New Year can come" he thought to himself, seeing the coming year as a beginning rather than another end. A chance to choose each step, each choice, knowing that as long as she stayed with him, whatever was to come his way, he was ready.

"Another drink?" he asked trying to distract himself from his thoughts.

"Yep, why not!" she replied.

As he stood at the bar he glanced over at her feeling as though he was definitely punching above his weight. As he paid for the drinks the barman responded with 'Happy New Year'

"Happy New Year!" he replied joyfully with a smile that came from deep in his soul.

The New Year began but he knew that this New Year was going to be different. In that moment he wanted to spend every day for the rest of his life doing just that. Returning to their table he placed the drinks down, deciding to take the seat next to her, instinctively their hands intertwined.

Too soon last orders were rung.

They left the bar stepping out onto the blanket of snow which lay on the ground almost deep enough to pass her ankles.

The snow continued to fall heavily as they walked through Tynemouth, with no idea how to get home, and neither wanting to leave, not wanting the night to ever end.

They continued to talk as they walked aimlessly in the falling snow. As they reached the park overlooking the Long Sands beach the snow began to turn to rain. Holding her hand Rob began running till they reached the old metal gazebo, taking shelter. Instinctively he removed his jacket draping it around her shoulders before pulling her close, his arms encompassing her to keep her warm.

They stayed in the gazebo watching the rain fall, remaining there for what felt like hours.

As the rain died, they continued walking. Walking her back to her apartment.

They stood in the doorway holding hands. She smiled looking up at him as though giving a silent permission to kiss her. She wanted so badly to invite him in wondering if he was thinking the same.

Frankie contemplated on how she had never taken a man back to her home on a first date but something about him felt right, as though they were meant to be.

He leant in kissing her lips softly and delicately causing her knees to become weak. His hand reached up touching her cheekbone before scooping her hair behind her ear with his hand ending behind her neck.

After a few moments in an embrace, they broke apart, Rob stepped back; his hands mirrored down her arms till he reached her hands, their fingers entwined.

He thought how he didn't want such a beautiful night to be tainted, he wasn't going to allow passion to take over, he was willing to wait to see if it was going to end the way he wanted, a new beginning, a beautiful night that would be the first of his forever.

"So what are your plans for New Year's Day?" Frankie asked trying to start a conversation to delay the goodbye.

"Erm... Work... I work at the hospice on the promenade... Then back home... That's about it..." he replied, his words trailing off followed by a silence.

"Well I guess I should bid you goodnight..." he uttered stepping back, his fingers slowly began parting from hers.

"OK, Goodnight..." Frankie replied before hesitating wondering what to say next.

Wondering whether to ask when they would see each other again, or to leave it and hope he would ring her, or whether to make the first move and ask him directly on another date.

"Look... I was wondering..." she spoke nervously before pausing.

The thought of him spending New Year alone tugged at her heart. Through their conversations earlier that night, he'd told her how he lived alone. She knew that being alone doesn't always inspire you to cook, to eat properly.

She took a deep breath before continuing.

"Do you want to come back tomorrow after work for a proper home-cooked meal? Cause you look like you need it" she smiled slyly.

"Yeah, why not... sounds good" he smiled as he took another step back, their hands parting fully.

His hands clung onto his thighs as though he didn't know what to do with them, as though they didn't know how to function when not connected to hers.

"Night.. See you tomorrow" he continued with his smile growing to the almost cheeky grin that she fell for that first night.

She entered the flat closing the door before standing with her back to the door smiling, she thought how whichever smile he gave melted her heart, whether that small shy smile or that cheeky grin which could light up any darkness.

She slid down the door till she was sitting on the floor reminiscing over the night, thinking how he was so lovely, and gentle and caring, and such a gentleman.

"Right!" she spoke to herself as she stood up, deciding she needed to get some sleep before getting up early to go shopping, her mind contemplating a million meal ideas, wondering what to make him and panicking, what if he doesn't like it?

Rob returned to his empty flat, walking out onto the balcony overlooking the river and the distant lighthouses.

He flicked through his phone seeing a message from Imogen, a message which he had missed.

Happy New Year... How's the date going?

He smiled as he replied.

I'm definitely falling in love! Seeing her again later... Talk soon.. Oh, and yeah Happy New Year x

Taking a sip of his hot coffee he couldn't help but wonder if that new day was going to be the first day of the rest of his life.

Chapter 3

6am. New Year's Day.

There wasn't time for sleep, and he knew that he wouldn't have been able to sleep even if he had the time. He was counting the hours till he would see her again, he just had to survive the 6-hour shift.

He looked out of the window contemplating whether to walk or if he could take Buzby which would allow him some more time, time for a shower and a coffee to give him the strength to push through. The snow was slowly beginning to melt creating slush.

"I've ridden in worse!" he told himself.

He rolled his shoulders wincing, his hand instinctively reached for his shoulder blade as he felt a searing pain shoot through his bones and joints. He knew the pain well, one of many symptoms to his kidney disease, and the worse his kidneys became, more related symptoms began to appear. He knew he just had to push through.

Part of his determination to not let his kidneys to define his life came from his stubborn-ness, seeing the need for help as a weakness, but also his mother's words constantly repeated in his head, he was lazy, but now he had responsibilities.

He flicked the switch on the kettle before walking towards the bathroom.

He stepped into the shower, his toes flinching as they touched the chilled ceramic floor. He turned the old metallic dial, releasing thousands of lukewarm drops of water waiting for the old system to kick in, for the water pressure to increase and become warmer. He stood lost in thought as he allowed the water to trickle down his back in the hope that it would awaken his senses, to give him a second wind. His eyes closed. His mind continued to tumble with thoughts and memories over and over, each time showing images of her like photographs, unable to escape the picture of her in his mind, not that he would ever want to...

He sat on Buzby while fastening his helmet. He lifted himself from the seat as he turned the key before kicking the kickstart, the bike returned a grumble.

"Come on old girl, don't let me down now.." he spoke out loud as he repeatedly pushed down on the kickstart with no avail.

"OK!" he muttered under his breath as he dismounted, wheeling the bike back into the small bike shed.

Removing his helmet, he patted the engine.

"It's OK girl, your just as old and broken as me"

Locking up the shed he looked down at his watch wondering whether he could get to work if he walked fast enough or whether to waste money on a taxi, knowing that the rate would be higher with it being New Year's Day.

He began walking heading through Tynemouth and along the coast, arriving with a few minutes to spare. The hospice overlooked the sea. As he walked up the steps the sun was beginning to slowly rise on the horizon.

He hesitated for a moment as his hand rested on the door handle. He closed his eyes tightly; his head was beginning to pound feeling as though it was going to explode causing him to feel nauseous.

He opened his eyes, pressed down on the handle walking in.

"Happy New Year Ladies!" he announced with a beaming smile masking his pain, something which he had become good at doing.

The shift felt longer as though time had slowed. 1pm he walked out of the hospice stepping onto the path. He stood staring at his phone before sending her a message.

Do you still want me to come round? I've just finished.

He stared at his phone, willing it to light up and buzz to indicate that he'd received a message, that she had responded.

Frankie stood in the kitchen with pans boiling on the hob, staring at the roast chicken in the oven she began wondering if he would turn up, thinking that maybe he'd change his mind.

Her phone vibrated on the kitchen surface. She smiled as she read his words. She hastily sent a reply.

Yes! I still want you to come around... I have a roast in the oven, and I can't eat it by myself.

Rob waited for what felt like an eternity. Waiting for his phone to vibrate indicating a message had been received. When it did, his body jolted as he unlocked his phone with delight, like a child unwrapping a candy bar. He wasn't let down. He read her reply, a smile crept across his face. He quickly replied.

I'm on my way.

"Right!" He declared as he began to walk taking deep strides desperate to see her again.

He stood outside of the apartment block scanning the buttons realising he didn't know what number she lived at. He let his fingers walk over the rough stone wall as though to allow himself some time to compose himself. He wanted so badly to see her but also was afraid of messing it up. It always felt as though his whole life was a myriad of mistakes.

For a moment he thought about turning and walking away. He took a step back as he thought how she deserved so much more than a loser like him.

Something made him fight against his thoughts, determined to not allow himself to fall to the depths of self-sabotage, to his default. The thought of never seeing her again was much stronger than the demons which consumed his mind. His heart was winning the battle within.

Taking his phone out of his pocket he dialled her number.

"Hi.. I'm outside..."

"I'll be down in a minute" She replied before hanging up.

He stood looking through the glass panel in the door frame, waiting. His heart skipped a beat when she came into view.

As she walked to the door opening it, she looked up at Rob. He looked tired; his eyelids had a slight yellow tinge which looked more evident against his almost greying complexion. She took his hand leading him up to her apartment.

They enjoyed dinner before sitting talking on her settee with a bottle of wine. Rob found himself opening up to her, talking of his daughter, the situation with her mother, and the strained relationship with his family declaring how he could never measure up to his mother's expectations. How he wasn't invited for Christmas, constantly feeling abandoned.

She could see the sadness in his eyes as though he was trying to hold back the tears. She wondered how anyone could make him feel so insecure. She had only just met him, but she could see that he was so gentle and caring.

He confided in her about his kidney problems, his failing health, his broken dreams. He'd only been that open, with one other person, finding it too hard to become emotionally vulnerable with anyone.

Too often he would hide behind his built-up walls but with Frankie it was easy and felt right. Something in her made him want to open up, to bare all as though she'd managed to penetrate his walls seeping into his heart and soul.

He paused wondering if he'd revealed too much, afraid his insecurities would begin seeping back, but hoping that she would still want him with all of his baggage, that she would still remain.

"Well, you have me now, you don't need anyone else" she stated as her hand took hold of his.

A calmness transcended different than any other time in his life, as though he had finally found somewhere to belong, he could just be. She didn't want, need or expect anything from him.

For a moment that feeling made him feel uncomfortable, vulnerable, he didn't know how to respond.

He stood up.

"I think it's probably time I headed home, to get sorted for tomorrow's shift."

She could see his insecurity written across his face.

He made her feel like she had known him forever and never wanted to be parted from him. She knew he would make the greatest carer, such a selfless soul though it was obvious that no one seemed to take care of him. She decided she was going to make sure he was looked after, cared for, loved.

Frankie's hand reached up taking hold of his.

"Stay…." She whispered.

"I'll run you a nice bath, and then after we can just sit here and relax, and I've got dessert..." she hinted hoping that the way to a man's heart really is through his stomach.

He hesitated for a moment. He felt as though he should go, that this new relationship should be done properly, but he didn't want to leave. He never wanted to leave.

He looked deep into her eyes; he pursed his lips as a smile began to escape. No-one had shown him that level of attentiveness and deep down he didn't want to be parted from her.

"OK" he replied.

"Right! Bath!" she exclaimed looking up at him wanting so desperately to kiss him, to kiss away all the hurt, all the pain.

As he lay in the hot bath he slid down into the water, letting it cover him, his body relaxed. He let out a welcome sigh. Back in his flat he only had a shower and back at his mother's house it was rare to have the opportunity for a long soak.

Frankie entered holding a fresh towel placing it upon the radiator trying not to look at him. He began to sit up as though to get out.

"I'm not here to rush you, take as long as you need, I'm just bringing in a towel for you when you're ready"

She turned looking down wanting so badly to look at him.

"Have I died and gone to heaven? I hope this is heaven..." he exclaimed.

She tried not to smile. Before leaving she couldn't resist taking a quick glimpse. Her lips parted as she inhaled deeply as she watched the water rolling down his hair softly. The water defined his perfect body.

He glanced over at her, he could see her trying not to look at him, her shoulders were shaking, her eyes were narrow slits diverting his gaze.

Her face slowly became bright red as a searing blush consumed her, her smile was so wide though she was trying so hard to disguise it.

Exhaling deeply, she walked out trying to compose herself.

After his bath they sat together drinking more wine and eating dessert.

The hours past, the sky darkened.

"I think you need a good night's sleep" she insisted, taking his hand, leading him to the bedroom.

She fell asleep soothed by the sound of his heartbeat.

As she lay in his arms he began to drift into sleep, feeling so close to her and safe in her arms, though he wished there was no clothes between them.

As he tried to fight his tiredness, he wondered what she saw in him. All his life he felt as though he belonged at the end of the line, that he was a nobody, that he never really felt as though he belonged anywhere, but it was as though she had rescued him. He thought how that day had been perfect and how it felt like the start of something more wonderful.

The first day of the rest of his life, something more than he could ever imagine.

He fell asleep having the first perfect night, feeling as though he was home.

Chapter 4

Slowly and reluctantly, Rob began to rouse while wrapped in the soft sheets, A new day had begun. He reached his hand out taking hold of the fabric as he nestled himself further into the warm, soft sheets while remaining glimpses of a dream replayed in his mind, a dream he didn't want to wake from. His eyes were still closed as he soaked in the warmth. He blinked, closing his eyes, and blinked again as the morning sun caused streaks of sunlight to filter in through the gaps in the blinds.

As he began to awaken, he became aware that it wasn't his room, it wasn't his bed.

"Was he dreaming??" He asked himself.

He felt as though he had to pinch himself wondering if his dream was actually reality. He turned his head to see the other side of the bed empty.

Slowly he began to pull himself from the bed, dragging his feet off the bed, watching his legs hover inches above the off-white carpet before sitting up and allowing his feet to press down on the warm soft carpet. He rubbed his knuckles onto his eyes, stretching his arms above his head while yawning. He pulled himself to his feet standing in his boxers.

He rubbed the remainders of sleep from his eyes as he walked over to the window and gazed out at the horizon; its vivid light extended across a rosy sky. He had looked out at the early morning sun so many times in his life but that sunrise, that morning was different, something more than just beautiful.

He found it strange and hard to comprehend, to find something so meaningful in something so every-day. He thought how it was not like the sun wouldn't rise, it had after all, been reliably rising every day since the beginning of time and would rise long after he'd left the earth.

He picked up his shirt, the material warm beneath his fingers from lying in the path of the sunlight. Slowly he began fastening each button before walking out of the bedroom through the small apartment. Walking into the open plan dining room which also encompassed the kitchen to the welcome smell of fresh coffee. He spotted her standing there.

She turned smiling.

"Morning... I was just making you breakfast" she welcomed him holding a coffee cup in her hand gesturing him to take it.

As he took the cup from her hand, he lent in kissing her delicately upon the cheek.

"Morning" He smiled.

Taking a drink, he thought how he was definitely in heaven.

He sat at the breakfast table continuing to watch her in awe as he was happily absorbed by a feeling of love that played in her subtle smile and soft gaze. He watched as she carried their breakfasts over, before sitting across from him.

For the first time he could see every day of his future and wanted it. Wanting to stay and be a part of her life, the two of them together forever. He wanted it more than anything he'd ever wanted.

As she began to serve the breakfast, she questioned him, asking him what time he started work, if he needed a lift home to get change and a lift to work.

"I don't have to leave till 9am" she replied when he stated it was too much trouble.

She wasn't going to allow him to fob her off with platitudes.

"Do you want me to make you lunch?" She asked as she began clearing the dishes.

"No I'm fine" he replied beginning to feal a little uneasy.

"Really, I can make you a sandwich at least..." She paused and gave him an inquisitive gaze.

She smiled, and something told him that she wasn't going to take 'no' as an answer.

She drove him home, he felt squashed in her small white mini. She pulled into the carpark at Knotts flats searching for an easy place to park in.

Rob laughed, muttering under his breath.

"Women drivers"

"Hey!" she replied.

Rob laughed failing to hide his amusement.

"I heard that!" she continued.

Rob raised his hands as in a gesture of surrender as she pulled into a parking space.

"Want me to wait?"

He didn't want to be an inconvenience, to hold her up. He wanted to say no, to free her from the obligation but those words didn't come out, instead they were replaced by other words which as he spoke became a shock.

"Why not come up while I quickly get ready?"

"Yes, OK" she smiled as she turned the key, turning off the engine.

Exiting the car, she looked up at the old block of flats. Her eyes scanned up at the six storeys. She had passed the old, colossal block of flats many times but had never ventured inside.

Rob followed her eyes...

"It's Ok I live on the third floor and there is a lift!" he spoke as he took hold of her hand.

They walked across the carpark towards the external door. The door was a dark red with previous layers of paint showing through in the parts that had chipped or blistered and fallen away. It was made of a strong metal. Black hinges spread halfway across the door. It had an almost rustic appeal. Inside the corridor and stair were concrete, the walls a dark grey. It felt cold an unwelcoming.

She watched as he lifted his hand against a small metal panel allowing the sensor to register his black fob key which activated the elevator. They entered. The doors slid shut and the lift began to climb to the third floor without stopping. The lift came to an abrupt stop jolting them closer. The door failed to open straight away, and in part neither wanted it to open. Rob moved closer to her, unable to resist kissing her as his hand reached behind her to press the button to prompt the doors to open. His hand hovered for a moment wanting to savour every second. As his finger pressed upon the button the door opened.

"Sometimes it just needs a reminder on what it's supposed to do" he laughed as he stepped back slightly, edging out of the lift, standing in the doorway to prevent the doors closing on them.

She followed as they walked along the old corridor which was open to the elements. She glanced over the concrete wall at her car below.

She thought how any higher she wouldn't be looking over, it wasn't that she had a fear of heights, she just didn't like them.

They entered his small flat. A narrow corridor led into a small living room. Rob walked past her towards the conservatory doors which opened onto a balcony.

"Make the most of the view while I get ready... it's one of the only good things about living here!" he stated as he walked away.

She stood looking out over the balcony to the view of the river as her hand skimmed over the black wrought iron railing which sunk into the grey stone wall. She thought how under blue and sunlit skies, the view would be wondrous, but that morning was damp and bleak. A light grey mist hung over the river below. She shivered, allowing her arms to encompass herself as though to give herself a warm hug. She turned looking back inside. She stepped forward, returning back inside before sliding the door back closed. Scanning the room, she noticed how bare the flat was.

She scanned the array of photos upon the shelf, pictures of a baby, a little girl, and pictures of him with another woman.

She began wondering who she was, feeling a hint of jealousy as she realised that she didn't really know him yet, but wanted too. She wanted to know everything and be everything to him.

Rob walked back into the living room standing behind her, his arms encompassing her,

"Your freezing!" he stated as his arms wrapped tightly around her giving a feeling like a touch of heaven, a warmth as his body seemed to become moulded to her own, as though they were meant to fit together, like finding the right jigsaw piece to become complete.

His body heat began to transfer to her warming her not just physically but also emotionally.

He answered the questions which were flooding her mind without her needing to ask.

"Well…... That is my daughter Katrina…." His face lit up with love and pride.

"That is me and my best bud Imi.. She's a story for another day" he continued, smiling while trying to contain a smirk.

"Oh and that's me with her and her husband Marcus... also a mate, he's a fireman... Apparently that makes girls go weak at the knees..." his laugh was unable to be contained, a laughter which was so free and pure.

He moved around towards her side, turning slightly catching her eye. She tried not to laugh but was finding she was unable to remain serious whenever she saw that cheeky grin which penetrated deep into her soul.

He stepped forward backwards, she turned slightly almost facing him.

He took hold of her waist and spun her round. They stood in a moment as though time had stopped. She became lost in his eyes.

He looked deep into her eyes before kissing her, wanting desperately to take that next step.

He stepped away from their embrace in a bid to control himself.

"Well I think we should head off or we'll both be late!" he declared looking away to avert her gaze in the hopes that his thoughts hadn't betrayed him.

She drove him to work. They sat in the car outside, neither wanting to be parted.

He stood outside of the car, his hands resting on the roof bending down looking through the open window.

"Do you want to come over tonight? I'll be home by 5.30..." she asked.

"OK" he replied smiling but trying to remain relaxed, not wanting her to know how much he missed her already when she hadn't even left yet.

After that day he rarely returned home, rarely leaving her side, together almost every day since that first date. Only apart on the occasional weekends that he was granted access to Katrina.

It was just over a month since their first date.

As he looked at his daughter, he thought how much he wanted Frankie to meet her imagining the perfect little family he'd dreamed of, he also thought that maybe it was time to introduce her to his family, though that was one experience he wasn't looking forward too.

Chapter 5

February

Frankie sat at the breakfast table lost in thought. She glanced over watching Rob prepare breakfast. There was a joy in how he did it, he was happily absorbed by a feeling of love that played in his subtle smile and soft gaze as he brought it over,

"Your breakfast is served" he stated cheekily as he placed the plates down on the table in front of them, sitting opposite.

Those mornings had become a part of the rhythm of their lives together, and she never wanted to have a morning without him. Though something played on her mind. She had plans to go to Greece for 2 weeks for her friend's wedding at the end of the month. She had kept putting it to the back of her mind.

The questions tumbled through her mind, how could she survive 2 weeks without him, would he feel the same?

"I'm supposed to be going to my mates wedding in Greece for 2 weeks at the end of this month…." She blurted out.

"But…. I don't want to leave you here alone, and I'll miss you like crazy… maybe I should cancel?" she continued allowing her thoughts to form into words.

"No, you're not cancelling on my account... I will miss you like crazy but you're going!" he replied, though she could read the sadness in his tone.

He was never going to deny her the opportunity, but he knew that every day apart from her there would be that pain of a piece missing, the piece God gave to him to complete him.

"Come with me" She declared, the words forming before her mind could catch up, but once those words left her lips, she knew there was no other way this was going.

"I can't... I can't afford a holiday" He replied in a despondent tone.

"I'll pay" she replied.

Rob stood gobsmacked.

"I can't let you do that, plus I don't have a suit or anything... The only suit I have was he one from Imi's wedding but it's a bit mothballed..." he answered still in shock at her declaration.

"You're coming, and that's that... I'll sort the suit, no more excuses" Frankie stated in a stern tone but with a caring smile playing upon her lips as her hand gently brushed his shoulder.

"Well, I guess that's me told... We're going on holiday! I guess I should dig out my passport" he smiled with his smile beaming before taking a mouthful of food.

"And while we're on it, I have something for you... A key... you spend enough time here you may as well have one" Frankie declared with a smile playing upon her lips.

She stood up walking to the unit picking up a small gift bag, before walking back, passing it across the breakfast table.

Inside was a key and a keyring, one half of a heart. That key was like a symbolic gesture, as though to say you belong, and to Rob it reinforced his belief that wherever Frankie was... He was 'home'.

He placed the key and keyring on his keys, his beaming smile evident.

Later that morning after Frankie had left for work, he meandered along to his mother's house to pick up his passport.

He placed his hand upon the door handle, taking a moment before entering. He hoped that the door would be locked meaning everyone was out, that way he could pass undetected. His keys lay in his palm ready... His eyes instinctively drawn to the new key. His hand pressed down upon the handle and with a little pressure the door opened into the porch which always carried the aroma of flowers and giving the perception of a welcome home, even upon the floor was a woven doormat, upon it the words "Home". He gave a small laugh as he stepped upon it and walked in placing his keys back in his pocket.

"Hello" he shouted as he walked through the passage, peering his head into the living room, which was empty.

He shrugged his shoulders before walking into the dining room, walking over to the cabinet, opening the draw which housed all of the important documents... Most importantly the passports. As his hands searched, he wondered why he still kept it there, maybe out of habit.

"what are you doing?" he heard his mother speaking in a concerned tone that he had become accustomed too. He turned to see her standing in the doorway looking at him.

"Erm, just getting my passport mamma" He replied his head slightly bowing like a child caught with his hand on the cookie jar.

"Why do you need your passport?" she interrogated him.

"I, erm.. I'm going on holiday with my girlfriend"

"Girlfriend? Since when have you had a girlfriend, is this how I find out? Are we not allowed to meet her?

"We've only been together since New Year.. And who is we? The Spanish inquisition?" he replied with a confidence that he managed to find from deep within, though knew his boldness would be shot down..

"Roberto! Mind yourself!"

"Yes mama" he replied quietly

"So I assume this girl is where you have been spending your time, we popped by your flat the other night to find it in darkness... do you not think it is too soon to be going off on holiday with someone you barely know? and how are you paying for this holiday" Rosa asked trying to plant doubt within his mind, covert in her language, a technique she had used so many times before, always part of her strategy to keep in his place, it was her subtle form of emotional warfare.

He placed his hand in his pocket, his head down. His hand instinctively wrapped around the keys which lay in his pocket, the metal and skin coming together, there was a warmth from those keys. His mind replayed to that key, igniting a spark as he let his fingers curl around them.

"It is not too soon, and if I'm allowed to be honest... It is really none of your business... But Frankie is paying, it is her friend's wedding." He answered with a confidence, his head held high, no longer bowing down.

Rosa looked on with contempt. She gave a small laugh, amused.

"Do what you must! I have no doubt you will get drunk and ruin this woman's wedding... Then this girl will see you for who you are."

She turned to walk away.

"Why is it you always expect the worst from me?" he pleaded. A question which he never got an answer.

He turned back to the drawer, reaching in, his hand gripping his passport.

He stood holding it in his hand as his mother's words replayed in his mind, wondering if maybe she was right. Frankie was too good for him and one day she would wake up to that realisation. He closed his eyes tightly as though to expel those thought and doubts which always threatened to consume him.

He saw Frankie's smiling face. The love.

"No! mamma is wrong" he whispered under his breath; resolute as sobering thoughts awakened a realisation deep within, as though that realisation awoken something deep within as though he were somehow drunk before. It was the realisation that he was so much more than his families views on him. The realisation that so many times those words had cut deep and causing a knee-jerk response which on many times proved them right, which only enforced their opinions. A never-ending circle. Something he was now going to break. Through Frankie's love he knew he was so much more.

He walked out, not saying goodbye.

Those next few days his ticket was bought and that weekend they went shopping for a suit. His mother's words still lingered, though he used all of his energies to push them to the back of his mind.

As he walked, he became resolute that he as going to contribute, even if in comparison it was small, or a kind of token gesture. They were a team. He was allowing himself to look forward to their first holiday together as a couple.

He returned back to Frankie's flat returning 'Home'.

Chapter 6

As their first valentines approached, he felt fuelled by his love for her. He was for the first time truly looking forward rather than just living in the moment, looking onwards as a couple, secretly planning the future to come. He was in love. He thought he loved her from the moment he met her, and in a way he did. Love at first sight. But he was beginning to realise that what he was feeling for her was deeper, the word love never felt enough.

All too soon she became someone whom he quickly missed whenever she wasn't there. His moods would rise on her return. Her little quirks soon became his favourite thing. Her azure eyes pierced deep into his soul and soon everything blue reminded him of them.

Until her, he didn't know what love was. Everything else was just a prequel, an appetiser, or preparation for the real thing. He never saw it coming.

He might have seen it coming if he'd paid attention, except he was too busy being swept up in the moment, spending time with her, lost in the moments to even notice the change in him.

He decided that he was still going to make that Valentine's one to remember. He funnelled his efforts into creative cuteness, making love-letters which he hid throughout the flat and creating daft romantic songs.

He had always seen Valentine's day as materialistic, a day for companies to make money, restaurants to hike up their prices. He knew he couldn't lavish her with expensive gifts, or all the many things she deserved.

By the time Valentine's day arrived Rob had so much planned. The night before he had strategically place the many love notes throughout the flat. He woke up early and rolled out of bed, moving softly and quietly he placed the final note beside her pillow before tiptoeing out of the bedroom quietly closing the door behind him then continuing to walk into the kitchen. He moved about the kitchen with the kind of smile on his face that couldn't hide the love that warmed him from within.

Twenty minutes later he had pancakes, raspberries and freshly squeezed juice on the side. He placed everything delicately on a tray with a single red rose and carefully walked back to the bedroom. By the time he got back to the bedroom Frankie was only just stirring. He laid the tray gently on the floor and leaned in for a kiss, feeling a tingle spreading from his lips.

"Darling, I've made you breakfast. Happy Valentines!" Frankie opened her sleepy eyes and a warm grin spread over her face.

"I have a few more surprises after this," Rob winked mischievously.

Frankie smiled with a mouthful of food.

"Not too expensive, I hope." Frankie asked as she leant forward allowing her hand to gently stroke his cheek.

It had only been a couple of months, but it was as if she knew him inside out. She knew how he worried about not being able to provide, and always felt as though he was never enough, could never give enough. She earned more than him, maybe many men would find that intimidating, Rob didn't, well not in that masculine way but she knew he wanted to give her the world, but to her she didn't need anything else, because she had him, she did have the world because her world evolved around him.

Her thoughts tumbled in her mind as she looked at his face. She thought how before she met him it had felt as though she had lost her entire world.

She'd spent almost 10 years trying to hang on to something toxic, and something so incomprehensible that looking back she questioned her behaviour. Pouring love into an abyss, and in return living in fear.

Remembering how her now ex-partner put his all into each strike. His brawny arm would recoil back pausing, as extending the moment, the fear, as she waited for the impact of his own hand. Crying wasn't allowed. If she buckled, he would tell her to stop, or he'd give her something to cry about. He meant it too.

Many told her to leave. Looking back, she wondered why she stayed but hindsight is powerful. In some crazy way she thought he loved her, and thought she loved him, but it wasn't till she met Rob that she knew what love was. The day Rex broke her jaw was the last time she allowed him to have power over her, the turning point, the door opening. Deciding that she wasn't going to live that way anymore. Giving her the strength to break away, but that came with the loneliness and the fear still present, jumping at shadows, trying desperately to rebuild her life after being left with nothing.

Her life felt empty as though just going through the motions, and the thought of another relationship had been far from her mind, but that night, there he was. The one that put her mind into a frenzy of sparks. There was something in those brown eyes that was so beautiful, so safe and warm. In just one look it felt as though she was "home."

She reached out and made the connection, and like God Himself had arranged it, he fell for her just as hard. That first day was etched into her mind. Other memories faded or became hazy, but that day remained clear as though it was yesterday. She remembered how they talked, just the two of them, she could still recall the feeling he gave her.

She wondered if he knew that on that day, he had saved her.

"No, my love, not expensive - just a lot of fun I hope." He joked interrupting her thoughts.

Following breakfast, they took a walk down to the coast, her hand in his. That valentine's day was skipping stones over the briny waves and sharing a flask of hot chocolate on the sea wall as they got lost in each other's eyes, with him wanting nothing but to have her in his arms as though he'd found his treasure. With her he was the richest man on earth.

As they looked over the horizon together, he thought how it had only been 2 months, but he knew for certain that she was the one, the one to stand with him in all of life's joys, but also the storms. He knew in that moment that all he wanted was to be close to her, to feel her heart beat next to his.

He watched an old couple walk past hand in hand, their love was obvious to the world around them. As he watched them, he wondered if that could be them in years to come.

Until Frankie he had never allowed himself to think about growing old, and with her, for the first time in his life he could see the chance for that kind of love... The love that they say doesn't exist anymore. The type that spans far longer than one lifetime, a love that is not only filled with passion and determination but is also a serenity in which their souls could dwell in forever.

But in the back of his mind was still that place. The place where dark thoughts dwelled formed from a lifetime of shadows. Voices telling him he was not worthy, he would never be enough for her, that this perfection wouldn't last.

It was taking all of his courage to fight against those thoughts, to fight his insecurities, to continually find the courage to walk into the light after a lifetime of shadows.

Frankie watched as Rob seemed to be lost in thought.

"You OK? You seem a bit lost there..." Frankie asked as her hand gently squeezed his.

He nodded as though still lost in his mind.

"Is everything okay, really?" She urged.

He turned, snapping away from his thoughts, back into reality, looking at her with his warm eyes.

"So long as you're by my side, everything will always be OK.." he answered before kissing her softly.

He'd never been into PDA's, maybe because of his parents, but with her he found that where they were never mattered, he just wanted to hold her.

They returned to her flat, cocooned together in the privacy of their own space. The simplest touch of her hand was all that was ever needed to ignite his mind into a frenzy of sparks, to feel alive, to feel loved, to be wanted, but also igniting a passion, feelings he'd never had before, and with time it only intensified, moving in ways they had never learnt but knew so well.

He held her gaze as though stealing the passion from her eyes in a way that only magnified the spark between them creating an intensity of his gaze that they both knew was the start of the inferno to come. Engulfing his senses, capable to steal away all of his worries as they became one with each other, allowing himself to become as vulnerable as a person can be.

In that moment being only alive in the present, all thoughts of past and future melted away. She was to him the medicine that was bringing healing, and though he was becoming addicted he felt safe because he knew she was equally addicted to him.

That day felt magical. It was by far their cutest day, but he knew he had a lifetime to make more.

The day came for them to leave for Greece. They made their way to the airport where they were joined by Frankie's friends. It wasn't long till he felt welcomed into the fold. Those two weeks were amazing, they were inseparable.

He managed to remove his mother's words from his mind, allowing himself to coma alive. He told bad jokes and danced with moves which humanity hadn't had the pleasure of seeing, and in her embarrassment, she'd never loved him more. The more she got to knew him the deeper her love grew. He was the kind of guy to ask her to guess which hand a gift was in, hiding his nerves behind an angel's bluff.

The days rolled into nights, intoxicated but not by alcohol but rather by the electricity which sparked from them. The intoxication that comes with real love. Intoxication which brought every fibre of his soul alive, bringing a state in which he never knew was possible.

She never wanted or needed anything with him beside her, he brough the joy, the excitement, the laughter but most of all the comfort and security she had never know. That attentiveness was a part of who he was and if she was honest, the most attractive feature she'd seen in a man.

Too soon the time came to leave, to return home.

Chapter 7

March.

The coldness of winter was being replaced by the warmth of Spring. Bringing with it the assurance of new life, new beginnings. They had over those past 3 months became a real couple, something that both knew was real, something that would last forever.

Frankie introduced him to her Mother and Father and they instantly fell in love with him, creating an instant connection, and in them he found the family he'd always wished for. She introduced him to her brother Brett, and in him he not only found a brother but also a friend. He had thought that with Imogen and Marcus so far away, and Charlie always so busy he had nobody, but Brett helped to fill that gap. It was beginning to feel as though his life was falling into place, everything perfect, that now he had all he ever needed.

Rob introduced Frankie to his mother. She was polite but he could see her looking her up and down trying to mask her disapproving face though it was evident. He thought she was either getting worse at keeping up pleasantries or that she was deliberately not concealing her feelings completely. He couldn't understand why she appeared to be apathetic to his partner.

She was beautiful, kind, caring, and not that it mattered to him she had a good job. He soon realised that it was due to Frankie not bowing down to his mother's superiority, Frankie could see through the fake façade and wasn't afraid to call her out on it.

He introduced Frankie to Katrina. The baby he had held in his arms was quickly becoming a toddler, quickly approaching her 1st birthday, and he soon realised she had his wild inquisitive nature.

They had a few magical days as a family, days at the park and the beach. Rob watched Frankie's eyes light up as she played with Katrina, and in those moments, it felt as though his dreams had come true, that they were a family. The rest of the world didn't exist, until he had to return her and the bubble burst.

He suffered backlash from his family as to them he introduced this new woman to Katina far too soon, though he knew even if he'd waited longer, they still wouldn't be happy.

One Sunday afternoon he walked into his Mother's house with Katrina in his arms. He could hear the conversation from the living room, the raised voices, the tone evident.

"What on earth does he think he's doing with my kid introducing her to his new bit on the side... I don't know her from Adam….. She could be anyone... Over my dead body is she going to think she can play the role of Step-mum….."

He heard his mother's voice replying as though to agree. Rob shook his head in disbelief sighing. He thought how it was OK to introduce her children, including his daughter to a string of men.

It felt like double standards, but he was beginning to expect nothing less, his life had been a string of double standards, he just wished for once his Mother would take his side.

He remained standing in the hallway as though in shock. They had no idea he was there listening. Katrina let out a laugh which caused the conversation to end abruptly. Raquel walked out of the living room into the hallway.

"What?!" Raquel uttered giving a scowl which spoke volumes as she took Katrina from his arms.

"I heard you, that's what!"

Raquel shrugged as though she didn't care.

"All I want is you to be fair! That's all I'm asking" Rob dropped his tone in the hope that she would be willing to see from his side though he knew he was fighting a losing battle.

"What on earth do you mean by fair?" She replied though having no intention of being civil, she just enjoyed getting him worked up, and having Katrina she knew she had the upper hand.

"What I mean is Frankie is my partner, and it's not like she's just some random off the street, I don't introduce her to God knows who... Unlike you! You can't expect me to stop Frankie from spending time with me and Katrina..."

"Yep! That's exactly what I expect!" she answered abruptly while raising her eyebrows.

"I'm sorry, but I mean it! I don't want her around my daughter" she continued.

Though he knew she was not sorry, in fact she was enjoying every moment, every ounce of control.

"OUR DAUGHTER!" Rob interrupted in a raised tone.

Raquel gave a small laugh trying to disguise the disbelief that he had dared to challenge her.

"MY DAUGHTER!!! And... if you can't handle that then you won't see Katrina either!" She continued, before walking towards the door.

"You're not serious" he uttered as her hand rested on the door handle.

She turned back slightly with a smirk creeping across her face.

"Deadly serious! It's her or Katrina, your choice!" she replied as she pressed down on the handle, opening the door, and walking out without a second glance.

Rob stood frozen. His mother walked out of the living room, he looked at her as though to ask why but she barely looked at him. He thought how he hadn't really expected anything else.

He walked out of the house, walking down the drive to his small car, his father's old car. He sat in the driver's seat looking in the rear-view mirror looking back at the house and down at the baby seat in the back seat.

"Dad, I wish you were here" he whispered as his head bowed, resting upon the steering wheel.

He struggled to make sense of the conversation, but what he was certain about was Raquel wasn't going to win. Frankie was the love of his life, his partner, his soul mate. He was never going to give her up for anyone, he was willing to fight, he'd given up on always giving in to Raquel.

He returned to the apartment and fell into Frankie's arms.

"What's wrong?" she asked with such sincerity.

He looked away as though the outside world had his attention, a deflection in the hope that he could pretend that everything was ok, but after all their time together she could read him like a book.

Her hand gently reached up to his cheekbone, her fingers delicately brushing his skin before allowing her hand to gently persuade him to reorientate his face until she could hold his gaze, his spark appeared missing from his eyes, there was no smile upon his lips.

He broke down in her arms as he told her of what had occurred.

He lay in her arms feeling as though a weight had been lifted.

Talking to her always brought a calmness.

He lay in her arms allowing his mind to feel unburdened, he thought how there was beauty in being a good listener, someone who seeks to make connections. From that first moment he met her he was drawn to her 'safe eyes', a beauty that was real, beautiful inside and out.

He thought how he loved all of her, her curves, her softness, but also her strength and her passion. She had a passion that could turn her eyes into orbs of the brightest fire, and in them he could see clearly that she would fight to the very last breath for him. She would not let the world break her or allow anyone to break him.

Sure, she could cry, but she would never let them win.

Slowly over those coming months Raquel and his mother began to conspire that he was unsuitable to look after Katrina, but he knew from hearing that conversation and from the not-so-subtle comments which were dropped into almost every conversation, that it was more so that Raquel didn't like Frankie fulfilling the role of stepmother, maybe allowing her insecurities and the realisation of her parenting skills causing her to form a deep-seated jealousy.

The tension led to a period where the weekends that he would usually have custody of Katrina, instead became weekends gaining 'access' with Katrina staying at his Mother's. Weekends where he visited under her supervision. He found the situation frustrating but was willing to fight, though decided to play the long game and pick his battles. He wasn't going to allow them to ruin his relationship with Frankie or destroy his happiness.

Some days were harder than others, one of those days was Katrina's 1st birthday. A day he found the multiple hoops he had to jump through too hard to comprehend, too hard to fight.

He thought how he had never really known what love was until that April morning in the hospital one year earlier, the day he held his daughter for the first time, the day he became a Father. She was his.

He stood outside his Mother's house holding a present in his hand. Pink banners covered the window and the door. As he stood there with his hand resting on the door handle, he remembered that day, the most perfect feeling he had ever known had swept through him. He was rocked to his core. He knew he would do anything in the world for her.

He would be her hero, the one who would give her endless cuddles and keep her safe. He would be her Daddy. As his hand pressed down on the handle and the door began to open, he could hear that sweet little giggle and it gave him enough resolve to never give in. He loved her.

He entered the house, the walls strewed with bunting and banners. The same bunting which was brought out at all birthdays when they were children... There was something about that old bunting that sparked joy, as though connecting the past with the present.

He entered the living room.

Katrina was sitting on the floor in a beautiful gold sparkly dress, gold sparkly shoes and a matching gold headband. She looked up in Robs direction and squealed with an excited look as her hands began to clap.

"There's Daddy's little princess" Rob whispered under his breath.

He walked towards her, dropping down to his knees. Her arms instinctively reached out as he leant forward, scooping her up in his arms. Slowly she was becoming a little person, no longer a baby, her personality was beginning to flourish and that smile always melted his heart.

The morning felt magical, and for a while it felt like family. The whole family was there. Isabella, Greg and Owen, and his Mother.

He could imagine his father sitting watching from his old chair, just like he used too, but he wasn't really there, he was missing... Just like there was also someone else missing....

The party was over far too quickly. He'd always been told to believe quality over quantity, but he still felt robbed, he wanted so much more, more time, and time alone without his family or Raquel watching from the side-lines.

Rob watched as Raquel was saying her goodbyes and thanking his mother for the gifts and the party, he watched her play the dutiful daughter. He could see right through her and could not understand how others couldn't see how fake it all was.

His thoughts were disturbed by a car horn.

"That's my queue to go" Raquel spoke trying to pick up all the bags.

"I'll help you" Owen gestured, taking the bags before walking out with Raquel following behind.

Rob followed. Owen walked ahead to the car placing the bags in the back seat giving a friendly gesture to the young lad in the driver's seat.

"Who's that?" Rob asked.

Raquel looked at him with contempt.

"None of your business!" she answered.

"How is it your trail of boyfriends get to be in Katrina's life, but my partner doesn't?" he asked.

Raquel shrugged her shoulders refusing to answer, instead she thanked Owen for his help before fastening Katrina in the car seat, waving goodbye to his mother who was now standing at the front door before climbing into the passenger seat.

Rob stood in shock as Owen walked past him, nudging him as though he was in the way. He continued standing on the pavement as thoughts tumbled through his mind. He turned towards the house, the door closed, everyone getting on with their lives as though he was invisible or unimportant.

He walked into the house picking up his jacket from the coat-stand.

He hesitated, wondering if he should go say goodbye, but he couldn't face them, the constant rejection and the disappointment was slowly suffocating him.

Chapter 8

Rob stood in Frankie's kitchen, though really with the amount of time he spent at her flat he could be mistaken into believing it was his kitchen.

"So what you wanting?" Rob asked casually as he moved around the kitchen with his iPad resting upon some cookbooks with Imogen on facetime.

"Where are you?" Imogen asked inquisitively.

"I'm at Frankie's"

"You moved in or something?" Imogen replied.

"Or something.... I spend enough time here, she trusts me with a key..."

Rob stepped away, turning his back slightly.

"What are you doing?" Imogen's voice echoed through the kitchen.

"I'm getting dinner ready for when Frankie gets home, and some annoying dance chick decided to interrupt...."

"Cooking?" Imogen laughed.

"Hey! If I remember correctly it was you that can't cook! We both know Marcus didn't marry you for your culinary skills..." he replied.

He'd missed their roasting of each other.

"Nah, we know he married me for so much more..."

"Ahem... Can we keep this convo PG?"

"Yeah, whatever old man..."

Imogen could see how relaxed, happy and content he was. As though he'd found his purpose in life.

"You talk... I cook...." He joked.

"So, you never said the reason for the call..." he asked.

She decided to deflect away from the real reason for the call. She couldn't say it was because she missed him, or because she was struggling. That the workload was overwhelming. That she just needed to hear him say 'everything will be OK'...

She thought how she needed to be selfless. He had been her rock for too long, she needed to be there for him, but more so, to stand on her own two feet. She needed to put him first, be there for him to even out the balance, she knew she had to stop relying on him to save her, to steady her...

"What!? Can't a girl check in on her so-called bestie anymore? I'm just checking in on you... And Kitt2... and Buzby.." She answered.

"So..... Kitt2...." Imogen continued.

Imogen had reluctantly left Kitt2 in his care, knowing that it wasn't practical to keep her with the move to London.

"That bike is possessed you know!" he replied sarcastically.

"Nah, she's just got a mind of her own, she probably misses me, you know she only ever behaved for me...... Well OK not always!"

Imogen laughed as she recalled some of the situations that she got herself into with that bike.

"Come on... don't keep me in suspense!" Imogen pressed for more depth, and the reasoning behind his statement.

"Well, Day 1. She gets a parking ticket.... Never in the history of riding have I ever got a ticket for a bike."

Imogen scrunched up her face and raised her eyebrows.

"Well that is more your bad parking than Kitt! Anything else to back up your claim?" Imogen asked trying not to laugh.

"This is a story and a half..." he started trying not to laugh as his mind began to recollect the events of the previous couple of weeks.

"We went for a ride with Ezzie and Billy to the factory estate... Billy was riding Kitt2... We went to the old factory estate so that Ezzie could have a go at riding... You know she's hoping to do her CBT soon... Well, as we begin trying to show Ezzie the ropes... and by the wayside... she was worse than you on your first go..." Rob paused trying not to laugh.

"Anyways.... The patrol guy then tells us he's phoned the cops 'cause it is illegal to practice bikes... So, we belt it off towards the off-road track.... Billy ended up pulling a huge wheelie with Ezzie on the back. Ezzie then ended up on the ground laughing.... It almost reminded me of the wheelie Kitt2 and you pulled on the Mount... Though this wheelie was even higher, so much so that the number plate broke! So, we ended up having to ride back without a number plate... We ended up with a cop van behind us... I screamed and bombed through the lights just before they turned red and bombed up back lane and back into the garage. Billy caught up with me saying Ezzie jumped off back near the lights. So laughing our heads off we hopped in the car to go find Ezzie.. When we got near the lights a jam car was patrolling, we assumed it was looking for us so headed into town to ring Ezzie to see where she was... Epic third date!!!! Do you think they'll make it to a fourth?" Rob paused laughing uncontrollably.

"Hmm... Well I blame Billy's riding... Not my girl... Do you have anymore evidence in your defence?" Imogen asked pursing her lips trying not to laugh. Hearing the exploits gave her an escape, even if just for a moment. Though listening to the stories made her miss the old life, especially the wild adventures.

"Ok... 2nd week we go back out... Billy ends up riding off on his own, I got stuck behind an old guy going at a snail's pace... Billy ended up pulling another wheelie. He reckoned Kitt suddenly picked up speed and pulled a wheelie of her own accord and she went flying out from underneath him.. He swears he was in 1st... He broke his arm... It is now in a cast... I have no idea how he managed to ride back to mine... Besides from Billy I have to point in defence that she continually floods petrol... The footrest is now broke... The kickstart lever is hanging on by a thread... The horn no longer works... I reckon we should change the plate to C666 GKO"

"Why the GKO?" Imogen quizzed.

"Gecko"

"OK, Whatever!" Imogen answered shaking her head.

"Wild as always.." Imogen continued with a drop in her tone.

"No, Don't you know I'm all respectable now... Billy is a bad influence... I think I'm getting too old for adventures like that... and I was never as crazy as that Billy!"

"You keep telling yourself that old man..." Imogen interrupted.

"And..... You getting all responsible?!" Imogen continued, laughing.

"Well I guess being a Dad and finding a good woman can tame even the wildest of men...." Rob stated.

"Anyways, about being a Dad... how was the birthday bash and stuff?" Imogen interrupted in an attempt to divert the conversation.

"The birthday was good; Katrina is growing so fast it is unbelievable!"

"But.... I sense a but......"

"Well the family were a nightmare but what is new there.... Raquel was playing her role so perfectly.... And Frankie wasn't allowed to be there, yet some jackass picks her up?" Rob sighed.

"I don't know how much longer I can keep this up, I'm getting tired of jumping through her hoops... She is unbelievable! Every time I disagree with her or I don't cave into her demands she threatens to stop me from seeing Katrina.... What sort of mother uses her kid like some kind of bargaining tool?"

"Yeah, and every time you let her get away with it you're effectively telling her that it's OK..." Imogen answered.

Her words were disturbed by an alarm as he began flustering around.

"You look a bit lost there... Proves my earlier point!" Imogen announced trying to lighten the conversation.

Rob could hear Imogen's voice as he pulled the dish out of the oven and placed it on the work surface.

"I wouldn't be if I wasn't constantly getting distracted..." Rob replied.

His reply was meant as part of their roasting of each other, it was a normal part of their relationship, but he was unaware that she took it the wrong way. She could feel distance growing between them, not just the physical distance but also an emotional distance.

Like other times her anxiety and her mind would twist his words creating a fake narrative which caused a feeling like an invisible blade being run around her skull.

He used to be able to read her like an open book, able to pick up on her cues, and put her gently back in her place, but the distance and all of the changes were making it harder. She could see him through the means of technology, but she still felt like he was a million miles away.

As she watched him, she wiped a tear from her eye. He turned back towards the screen. She composed herself, hoping he wouldn't notice, or in part hoped he would and give that reassurance which he had always provided in the past.

"So anyway, you were saying I should fight back? You do know I've got far more to lose..."

"You've got more power than you think..." She continued bluntly.

"Look, you want to be in your daughter's life, you deserve to be in her life, she is lucky to have a Dad like you... You know you've got rights too; the ball isn't always in her court.... Try calling her out on it..."

"Look, I've got to go... Marcus will be in soon and you've got your hands full there..." Imogen spoke as a distraction.

"But, keep in touch..." She finished before ending the call, not giving him a chance to reply.

He stood puzzled at her shortness, but soon became distracted by trying to get the remainder of dinner finished in time.

He looked at the clock... 4.55pm. He rubbed his hands together as he walked to the front door knowing she would be arriving home soon. He had waited at the door for her one day to greet her, but soon it became routine. Some days he would have a bath ready for her, sometimes filled with bubbles and scented candles. He wanted to treat her like the queen she was. He knew from conversations that her previous relationship was far from a bed of roses.

He watched her pull up. He opened the door in anticipation. As she approached, he opened his arms for an embrace. She fell into his arms feeling the warmth of her cheek next to his, feeling his soft hand brushing her hair from her face. Seeing his cheeky smile and his cheeky laugh in her ear... In his arms she could feel all her troubles fall away.

She had never received such love from anyone else. It felt great to be loved. He provided peace and serenity. He knew her better than anyone, loved her more than anyone, and even under that everyday monotony his love was always there: warm, cosy and just as real. Their body chemistry was off the charts, two apparent opposites coexisting as though one, as though two parts of one soul.

They sat snuggled together on the settee watching TV, though he wasn't really watching, his mind was replaying the day and Imogen's words.

"You've got more power than you think... "

He also thought back to dinner and Frankie stating the same ideals but using different words. He felt so thankful to have her by his side, she had become his rock. With her beside him he felt he could do anything, achieve anything. A pure gem of genuine honest affection with a unique affinity as though connecting their souls.

He thought back to that first night and thought how it was as though he found his missing piece, making him feel complete, as though he'd found the one his soul had been looking for and that he knew he'd found that missing piece the second he saw her.

His thoughts continued to tumble, thinking how great it felt to be loved, how it always felt so right in her arms. Before her, he always felt isolated and alone, on his own in the world where it felt as though no one genuinely cared for him, was never anyone's number 1.

With her in his life it felt like good things really could happen to a nobody like him. She made him a better man. With her love it felt as though he could rise above any obstacle. He began to believe in himself. He was beginning to thrive in ways he had never realised were possible. He was becoming more.... A better version of himself, yet still being himself, not feeling the pressure to change...

He was beginning to realise that when a good lover loves you, it's all good. He was becoming sure that they were right for one another. He resolved to fight, for once he wasn't going to continue to roll over.

Before heading to bed, he sent Raquel a text.

Meet me at the Priory, tomorrow 11am!

That following morning, he tried to compose himself. He looked in the mirror wondering whether he could bluff his way through. He was going to demand fairer access and use the threat of court.

11.15am he watched her standing, staring at her phone. He could see the frustration across her face.

As he approached, she looked at him with the look of contempt which was becoming shown far too often.

"You asked to meet up... then you keep me waiting!" she exclaimed coldly.

"Sorry, I just needed to get straight in my mind what I wanted to say to you..."

"Just say it... I haven't got all day! I have got a life you know, unlike some" She continued.

"We have a kid together...."

Raquel interrupted his sentence with an inpatient tone.

"Yeah and.... Where is this going?"

"I want you to cut me some slack. I want you to understand that Frankie is a big part of my life so deserves to be in Katrina's life... "

"Seriously... This again?" she answered as though she was bored.

"She is my family... I'm going to marry her...... She will be my wife whether you like it or not... You have no right to dictate who is in my life..." Rob continued hoping she would see sense and be reasonable.

"You've asked her, have you? She must have rocks in her head to say yes"

He wasn't going to answer that he hadn't asked her yet. Her comment began to play in his head.

Raquel gave a smile, feeling proud that she had such control.

"You really are pathetic..." she continued with a look of condescension as she began to step away.

Frankie's face flashed in front of him, the love so evident gave him the strength to fight back.

"We're not finished here!" Rob declared with an assertive tone as he reached out and caught hold of her arm.

"I don't know how many times I have to tell you this but it's not up to you... I'm Katrina's Mother!"

"And I'm her father!" He shouted,

"You're giving me no choice..." He continued.

His reply threw her, he'd never fought back.

"What you talkin' about" she replied trying to remain composed but panic was beginning to consume her like a flood.

"I'm talking about going to court! Getting official access to my daughter... Access that you won't be able to take away!"

His declaration made her feel like she was drowning, like she had been kicked in the gut. Courts meant social services; she didn't know if she was OK opening that can of worms. She walked away refusing to answer, for once speechless.

He knew he'd won that battle, he just had to stay strong and make her believe he would go all the way.

A few days later Raquel rang him.

"So we going to sort some schedule of access out or something"

Rob smiled knowing he'd won that battle but knew he had a long way to winning the war.

Eventually over the following weeks Raquel began to recede in her control of how and when he could see his daughter, and slowly he began to again have real access with his daughter, and access with Frankie.

Chapter 9

It was 7 months since he met Frankie. The summer was in full swing. Life seemed perfect. He spent his days when he wasn't working, out on Buzby, spending days with Katrina, but above all spending as much time as possible with Frankie.

Although he still had his flat it felt as though he rarely spent any time there. A few months earlier she had given him a key to her apartment and many days he would find himself at her apartment before she returned home, tidying making the house perfect and many nights she would return home to a cooked meal and sometimes a bath prepared with candles and flower petals. He would wait by the window for her to return, standing at the open door as she walked down the drive, there with open arms.

She'd never been taken care of like that by anyone, to Rob his only mission in life was to make her life wonderful, he couldn't give her riches, expensive gifts, but he could give her every piece of his heart and dedicate his life to making her feel loved and feel like a queen, because to him she was.

Over those past 3 months he had begun saving, his plan to save enough money to buy a ring, to be able to propose, to ask her to marry him, hoping her answer would be yes.

He awoke one morning in her bed. The night before was one of those nights where he lavished her with a romantic bath, a perfect evening. Frankie had left for work leaving him to sleep. His mind was focused on the fact that it was her birthday the next day. His mind was too pre-occupied that he'd forgotten about his hospital check-up that afternoon till a reminder flashed upon his phone.

He shrugged his shoulders. Those appointments had become routine, and over the past few years nothing had changed, it felt as if he just had to go through the motions.

He sauntered along to the hospital; Frankie's flat was only a 5-minute walk. As he walked, he was lost in thought at how perfect his life was, he was the luckiest man alive and he couldn't wait to ask her to marry him.

He sat in the waiting room, as usual the clinic had over-run. His phone kept ringing… Raquel… He thought how she could wait.

He thought that the only thing that threatened to burst his happy bubble was her and her incessant calls and demands…… Or so he thought!

He turned off his phone as the nurse called his name.

He sat in the small consultation room looking intently at his Dr who was staring at the computer screen at his recent test results.

He'd been in that seat so many times over the years waiting to hear of how his life became define by blood tests, BUN, creatine levels, and GFR, results showing the build-up of waste products in his blood, all which pointed to a percentage of his kidney function.

He could read it in his face, but in a way, he knew way before he walked in that it wasn't going to be good news. Luck had been on his side for a couple of years, his levels remaining pretty steady. He'd began the art of learning to accept the inevitabilities of his condition, becoming resigned to the inevitabilities of his future life without letting it continue to affect the present.

He thought how he had let it consume him over the years and there had definitely been dark days, especially in the beginning, but he was learning to accept things and go along with the changes that life asked of him, but without surrendering to them. Life was good albeit like climbing uphill, and now he had someone to climb with.

He continued to watch his Dr and began thinking how he'd began to notice that he was getting more tired, some days the fatigue being too hard to fight, and even harder to hide. His Dr turned to face him. He sighed before beginning to speak.

"It's not good news I'm afraid..."

The following conversation was like a blur, as though it was a dream.

It felt as though his world was falling apart just as it was beginning. It was a shock seeing his bloods indicating some renal changes including a drop in renal function. He walked out of the hospital in a daze, the numbers replaying in his mind. His GFR had dropped to 34ml, his kidney function being 38%, in stages of the disease he'd dropped down to 3B, having previously been steady in 3A. He seemed to be in autopilot, walking back into Whitley. As he entered the town, he walked through endless streams of people. People hurrying by like they were going to accomplish something, all with their lives ahead of them.

Lost in a daze he kept walking. He found himself in the Bay, staring at the pint in his hand, thinking how maybe his crazy lifestyle over the years had contributed, but back then he just wanted to live life to the max, make the most of the time he had and leave the world with a bang. He thought how his life was never easy, he thought his life was turning around, he'd found someone he loved, and she loved him back in return, someone who put him first in everything, but just as he thought he was getting his happy ever after the ticking time bomb showed that time was not on his side.

He felt like screaming at God, asking why? His faith had waivered over those many years but even so, he felt let down. Did he not deserve happiness??

He began to think of what his future would entail, the future which could be only a couple of years away. Dialysis, and transplant... Not wanting her to have to see him like that, to practically become his carer.

He thought how she said she would be with him all the way, but did she realise what she was signing up for?

He took a drink, and then didn't stop, as though trying to cause self-sabotage. That one led to many more as he tried to numb his emotions.

As he looked out across the bay, he thought how the tide was turning, not just in the sea but his life, his health... His levels had remained pretty much constant for quite a few years, not perfect but liveable, and good enough to push it to the back of his mind.

The symptoms ever present but mild and he'd learned to just cope with them, but now the tide was coming in, his levels had increased dramatically, now he could no longer hide from his future. His future felt like an unwalkable road, a journey into a land devoid of hope, a journey he didn't want Frankie to have to follow him into.

As he left the Bay, he meandered up to his mother's house passing the off license. He stood looking up wondering whether to go in, his thoughts fighting. He gave in, as though he was giving up... He walked in buying a few bottles placing them in his rucksack.

He entered his mother's house, his mother and brother Owen looked down on him with disgust which was visible in his eyes. It was obvious he had been drinking, and he didn't seem to care if they knew, he'd spent so many years trying to be perfect and normal but still never measured up.

"What you doing here? dropping off your washing?" Rob asked sarcastically.

"I could say the same to you since you don't live here anymore... Actually, mum and I had Katrina today.... Seems Raquel couldn't get hold of you.... You know I quite like playing a father role to that lovely little girl, especially since the father she got is a useless drunk!"

His mother stood in silence.

"I had a hospital check-up, that's why she couldn't get hold of me... I'm not at her beck and call, did she want to go find her next victim.." He let his words just fall from him.

"Aah, the old hospital excuse... It's getting a bit old, and also how many career changes have you had? And what is your job now? wiping arses! You're a joke mate...."

There was a pause which felt as though it could last forever, a silence in which you could hear a pin drop, but then the silence was broken as Owen continued.

".......and I guess that is also your excuse for the state your in... I wonder how long this lass of yours will stick around after seeing you like this!"

"Maybe that's for the best!" Rob exclaimed as he staggered up the stairs to his old room.

He collapsed on the bed, the room hadn't changed, it was just a little more 'empty'. His mind became filled with dark thoughts that he couldn't fight. He was no longer in control. The guilt, the fear, the overwhelming feeling of failure combined with the pain caused his mind to conjure a million excuses to cave in, to give in, to escape and numb the pain and silence the voices... As though taking a quick fix in the never-ending search for comfort.

He reached into his bag pulling out a bottle. He struggled to unfasten the lid, wondering if maybe that was a sign, that God was trying to tell him something, but that day he wasn't listening, he continued to drink till there was no more, slowly drifting away.

Frankie stood in the flat frantic with Rob's phone constantly going to voicemail. She knew he had the appointment that day. Her mind was creating a myriad of possible scenarios. The nausea swirled unrestrained in her empty stomach.

She scanned her phone. She hesitated wondering whether to ring his mother. At first, she resisted but as the hours past she felt it was her only option.

She listened to the dialling tone. His mother answered.

"Hi It's Frankie... You don't happen to have seen Rob?" she asked trying to mask the fear in her voice.

"Yes.. He's here!" his mother answered with a tone of disappointment.

"He's gotten himself into one of his states. He is drunk... Give him a day or two to snap out of it. Or if you know what's good for you, you'd cut your losses..." Rosa continued as though trying to show some concern for her.

Frankie was struck by her words and her tone. Her tone of voice made it sound as though it was normal behaviour, like she never did expect anything else.

The reality was that his mother had seen him get himself into that state far too many times, though never really asked or understood why, and never took any responsibility.

The following morning Frankie decided she wasn't going to take no for an answer, she wasn't going to allow them to keep him from her. She sensed something was wrong for him to end up there and in the state they claimed he was in. She had to see him for herself and was willing to listen and to understand if what they said was true.

As she was about to leave, she received a text, an apology with a get out clause. He claimed that she was too good for him, she deserved better.

He hadn't counted on her determination to fight for him, she wasn't going to let him give up so easily, she could read between the lines, his text seemed so dark and final, it just made her even more determined, she was willing to fight, willing to break down doors if needed.

She stood knocking on the door loudly. Rosa answered shaking her head in disbelief. Frankie could see Rob standing in the corridor, the colour absent from his face as though he could drop dead right there, and in Rob's mind until that moment that he saw her, it would have been what he wanted.

Frankie pushed past his mother taking hold of his hand pulling him towards her.

"We're going! No arguments!" she stated with a confidence that portrayed that she was taking no prisoners.

"I'll just get my stuff" he answered like a school child being reprimanded.

Frankie waited patiently refusing to make eye-contact with Rosa, refusing to engage in conversation as a feeling of contempt began to grow for his mother and his family.

As Rob walked back down the stairs, he watched her standing resolute. She looked up at him and her expression changed to that of a look of love and compassion. He smiled. He was always in awe of her confidence, her assertiveness, knowing when to be firm with him, and when to let him find his own way out of the pit holes he sometimes found himself in.

"Come on" she beckoned as he reached the doorway.

Taking his hand, she turned and began walking away failing to acknowledge Rosa.

Rob opened the passenger door of her little mini, tossing his bag into the backseat before climbing in, fastening his seatbelt, waiting for her to start the car.

He sat in silence as she sat with her hands firmly on the wheel. She turned her head slightly to flick her hair off her shoulder. Shrugging her shoulder she adjusted the mirror before starting the engine, pulling away, driving along the coast towards the lighthouse.

She parked the car in the carpark looking out over the lighthouse.

"Right! Now what's going on? Together we can take care of everything we need to... " She uttered confidently though her emotions didn't reflect her tone.

It was her birthday and deep down she was broken that the day had been overshadowed, but her love for him was stronger and ran much deeper. She knew she had to be strong, something she had learned over her life. She knew strength wasn't being free of fear, but in fact quite the opposite. Knowing that being strong is seeing all the issues and problems with no self-deception, no soft filters, anxiety in full measure, but hidden from view, acknowledging the fear. Going forwards doing the very best for others, and considering the self at a lower priority, to protect the ones she loved.

To be able to say, "I believe in you." When the world is trying to say otherwise.

He fully opened up, no holding back, as though truly becoming naked revealing internal scars which were buried deep within, the mess, the fear. She listened intently, no judgement. The one to wrap him in her unconditional love.

Still, she let him come closer, as though creating a sanctuary within her arms, letting him return without shame, an acceptance he'd never known.

"Whatever you face, we will face together... I will always be by your side, I will never leave you, never abandon you. Never give up on you... but in return you have to believe in me... in us and trust me."

It wasn't just her words; it went far beyond that which speech could ever accomplish.

She had been his lover but he was wakening up to the realisation that she was also his emotional support, his solid wall that he could cling to. When he couldn't stand alone, she was there to support him, to hold him up, to say "I've got you".

To help carry his burdens when necessary, and to never judge. He felt safe with her.

She was like a light of compassion and love breaking through his walls, bringing light into the darkness. With her filling him with love and an emotional warmth which made him feel stronger, almost invincible, as though all his worries just fell away, they weren't important. She gave him the courage to hold on, to keep going, but most of all to look forward to their future, that together they could conquer anything, even failing kidneys.

Her love was enough to save him, it just took time to trust, to allow himself to feel deserving, to weigh into it. In that moment it was as if his eyes were opened. He could see so much more, he could see so much more than can ever be explained, that sense of love.

He knew he had found the one, a blessing sent by God, someone he felt safe with and able to imagine spending eternity together.

It was as though her love brought an awakening.

The results and prognosis still hung in the back of his mind, but he managed to almost place it in a box and lock it away, knowing that his fate wasn't written in stone, there was no timeline anymore there was just 'now' with her by his side. He saw that moment as a turning point.

It dawned on him what day it was. He had planned to spoil her, but instead he had caused her so much worry and heart ache. He vowed to himself that was never going to happen again.

He had made it through many dark times but now it felt like the world was in his hands, a chance to start again, determined to be the man she deserved.

He had never really thought of "forever" before that moment. Now he could see his forever in her eyes. It made him even more determined to value every moment with her and even more determined to get that ring and give her a proposal that she deserved.

He began to plan that proposal, and to put those plans into action.

He found a ring, put down a deposit with the money he had already saved and began paying the remaining balance each week.

He knew it would take months but that just gave him the time to put his plan into action.

To become the man, he knew she deserved.

Chapter 10

The following months were like a rollercoaster. There were weeks and months where Raquel was almost normal, allowing access, at times even acting civil, creating an arrangement where they had Katrina for the weekends. Then there were periods of time where she would fly off the handle at the smallest thing, declaring time after time that he would never see his daughter again.

There were days that he felt as though he didn't have the energy, finding working difficult. He began to cut down his working hours, the strain from his health and the emotional strain at times was too much. It wasn't long before that news filtered back to Raquel who tried to use it to her advantage as though leverage.

Although each time broke him and he struggled being parted from his daughter he knew that her mood would soon pass, that access would be resumed.

Every day that he had travelled to work he found himself passing the old church overlooking Longsands, the iconic French gothic styled church which sat like a beacon. He often wondered if maybe one day he should wander on in, to talk to God, to thank him for sending Frankie to him, but too often he struggled feeling unworthy, the burdens too great, feeling abandoned. He hadn't stepped into a church for what felt like forever.

One afternoon following work, a month after that Dr's appointment he found himself walking through the graveyard, walking through the old wooden doors. The emptiness had almost completely left him. He fell to his knees as he talked to God.

"God, I know you're there" he whispered as he felt peace. He had found a renewed faith. He could see the light in his life, he could see hope, a renewed strength built on the resolve of the promises he'd made to himself in her car to be a better man for her, for Katrina, and for God.

When he felt like he couldn't take anymore he could see that little face, those little hands reaching up, and also just had to look to Frankie and he knew everything would be OK.

He began to see that Raquel got satisfaction out of seeing him broken, as though all being part of some sick game she was playing. He began to find that not reacting was the better strategy.

In the times when access was removed, they planned day trips and weekends away, to make the most of time alone, time to energise, to find the momentum to keep fighting the onslaught of negativity.

They went on many daytrips and short holidays to places like Scotland, but also Scarborough... Back to the place he still regarded as home, a place that would always have a special place in his heart.

He wanted to show her... To reminisce, to ignite some of the fun and craziness that the little town always managed to create.

They travelled down by coach as part of a coach holiday. She wouldn't drive those roads, his father's car was falling apart, and he knew wouldn't make the journey, especially the climb up Sutton bank. She was too scared to get on the back of Buzby, and Buzby would never carry all of their luggage.

He found the bus journeys to be one of the best parts of the trips, with it not being purely about reaching a destination, nor the arrival. The journey was about the travelling, quality time with his travelling companion, and a chance to kick back and to make new friends.

On the bus journey down to Scarborough he glanced out of the window as the coach rocked from side to side as they travelled those familiar roads, roads he had travelled so many times.

He looked around at the other passengers. Some had absorbed themselves in music, others engaging in short conversations with the strangers sat next to them. Altogether, all going to the same destination but all different. Rob turned, beginning a conversation with those behind, those sitting in front, then those sitting on the other side of the aisle until his infectious nature enveloped the whole bus. It felt as though everyone was engaging in conversation, the voices blending together in the sweet ritual of friends yet unknown.

Wherever they went they made friends, it was as though anyone who came into his orbit was captivated by his nature. Something Frankie was always in awe of.

They stayed at the Grande. He'd always wanted to stay there. Back when visiting Imogen they would enter the foyer just to stand on the red carpet, but now he was standing on the red carpet as a guest and it made him fee on top of the world.

Rob came alive dragging Frankie from place to place, becoming like a big kid in the amusements. Rob watched weary-eyed teens that he guessed were freshers at the university which sparked his memories back to those days. They seemed to be a lot younger, though he thought maybe it was him getting older. As he placed a coin in the slot of the claw crane machine, he caught his reflection in the glass. His scrawny figure had almost doubled due to being well fed. He felt like a blob... The word Blooby popped into his mind. Mr and Mrs Blooby, he laughed to himself... Though they weren't Mr & Mrs yet! He still had four months of payments before the ring became his and if he was lucky enough for her to say yes they could take that step to forever.

He snapped back to reality and began moving the claw slowly into position to win her a teddy bear. A few goes later his jammy luck again prevailed. He turned with the bear in his outstretched arms.

"For you!" he beamed like a proud child.

"Come on!" he continued not giving her a chance to react or reply running along the promenade to the ghost house.

He took delight in knowing that she had no idea what he was dragging her into.

"It's not scary, trust me" he declared with a cheeky smirk beginning to creep across his face.

He kept pulling her closer and closer,

"Are you sure it's not scary?" she asked.

"Nah, it's for kids, honest" he replied feeling a little guilty, though it was only a small white lie.

As they entered and began walking through the corridors, she clung to him, terrified as she screamed. Wanting to get out.

He began to bite the edge of the smile in a failed attempt to keep the creeping grin at bay. The smile escaped before growing into a giggle which continued to grow until he fell to his knees laughing. His laughter was so free and pure, like an innocent child.

"I'm sorry" he exclaimed as he managed to bring his amusement under control.

He returned to his feet pulling her in close, softly kissing her head.

I'm sorry, I love you, do you forgive me?" he asked with that puppy dog expression she could never resist.

"I hate you!" she exclaimed though failing to keep a straight face.

"Come on, just hold on tight to me and we'll get out in no time, I'll protect you" he stated pulling her in close trying to hide his amusement talking in a sincere tone, delighting in her falling into his arms as though for protection.

She continued to walk through the rest of the ghost house with his arm tightly wrapped around her, most of the time with her eyes closed allowing him to guide her. She thought she had gotten through it, but as they entered the final corridor and the door closed behind them, a masked man brandishing a chainsaw appeared.

Frankie screamed running towards the exit, falling through onto the path outside, those waiting to enter watching in amusement.

Rob walked out behind her calmly as though it was nothing. He looked over at the lads sitting at the desk who had been watching their exploits on the camera.

There smirks and laughter felt contagious and again Rob couldn't help but fall into a state of hysterics. His laughing was like ripples in a still pond after a stone had been thrown in, radiating outwards to everyone waiting, who had up until that moment been quite silent. All to soon the ripples of laughter became great waves of hilarity.

Rob composed himself as he looked at Frankie who stood unamused at his antics, though slowly the laughter was beginning to soften her demeanour.

Rob stood with his head down biting his lip, like a school child being reprimanded. He knew she would not forget it for a long time, but it had definitely been worth it!

A family joined the queue just as they began to walk away.

"What's it like?" The mother inquisitively asked as her young children ran around her, with one pulling at her arm impatiently.

"Don't go in! It's scary!" Frankie declared.

The little boy pulling at his mother's arm declared confidently

"I'm not scared!"

Before pulling his mother closer to the paying booth, turning to pull a cheeky face at Frankie as he walked in.

Chapter 11

January. A year after they first met.

Two weeks into the new year. A Thursday afternoon.

He walked along the coast; the onshore breeze was bringing a mild air rather than the usual winter chill. He thought how that January a year earlier was much colder, remembering the snow on that first date, but even though the winter was colder that year, it was the year his heart melted.

He began thinking back over that year, how back then he could never have imagined being where he was now. Thoughts and memories tumbled through his mind. Remembering their first Christmas together.

It was the first Christmas he truly felt a part of it rather than on the outside.

He smiled as he remembered that first Christmas together just a few weeks earlier.

He had access to Katrina the two days running up to Christmas Day.

Days where they created memories. Memories to keep bottled inside to keep him going when the journey got tough.

Frankie had filled the apartment with silver packages for Rob and Katrina to find. It felt magical. Rob had never known Christmases like that before. Frankie loved spoiling them both with those days feeling like a real family.

Rob came alive as though in his element. He dressed as Santa to bring Katrina her presents. She stood on tiptoes reaching up to the window ledge, eyes wide, hoping to see Santa arrive down the path, not on a sleigh but on a tinsel covered motorbike.

As she heard the roar of the engine and saw that bike pull up on the car park outside, she began to jump up and down excitedly, giggling like only a young child can with an infectious kind of laugh that lights up everyone, like an echo of the children they once were.

"Daddy!" she squealed recognising him underneath the red suit and fake white beard.

Frankie scooped her up carrying her downstairs, opening the door. She ran towards him, arms outstretched giggling, waving her arms for the pick-up she knew was coming, being hoisted high in his arms.

He took the role extremely seriously, riding around the surrounding streets throwing sweets and chocolates at wide eyed excited children, perhaps enjoying it more than the children themselves.

Children's laughter filled the streets.

Frankie watched with Katrina in her arms loving seeing him so happy, that happiness just made his love greater, magnified in everything he did. As she watched him park his bike and walk towards her, kissing her upon the cheek, looking happy and content and proud of the joy he had brought, she thought how they say you can't bottle love. To her that was untrue. Rob was the proof with that bouncy stride of his, his emotions that slowly tiptoed out. His warm loving care-free smile, his generosity and especially every hug emitted love.

She wondered how many of those who were touched by him went on to become better friends, better bosses, better parents, and above all better people because of the care and the love spreading out from just one man. Knowing that just seeing him made everyone in his orbit glad to be alive.

They shared a magical Christmas dinner with the table adorned with Christmas crackers tinsel and candles. Katrina bounced in her chair dancing to the Christmas music which fill the room. Swinging her legs in the air, clearing the floor by several inches as they swung back and forth as her head and arms went up and down, while her face was a picture of concentration.

After dinner they at together as a family as Rob read to Katrina by candlelight taking great joy in bringing the stories to life with different voices and elaborate actions with laughter in his eyes and a smile twitching at his lips.

His imagination took over as he began to recite stories which had begun to forge within his mind.

It felt like perfection, like how life was meant to be, the perfect little family. The clock chimed breaking Rob's contentment knowing it would be over all too soon.

Late Christmas eve, Owen arrived to pick up Katrina to take her back home, back to Raquel.

Katrina cried, arms outstretched towards Rob as Owen carried her away wanting to stay, to spend all of Christmas with Frankie and Daddy.

Rob felt his heart tear watching her so distressed wishing she never had to leave. He also knew the tears and tantrums would anger Raquel. That she would be jealous, that she would claim he had deliberately tried to outdo her.

Though to Rob, Katrina wasn't a porn in a game. He wanted to make her happy for her, not for some sick game of one-upmanship.

He continued to walk picking up his pace as he turned, walking inland up into Tynemouth Village. He thought back to New Year's Day, just a couple of weeks earlier.

The anniversary of 1 year together. It was simple, just being together, both content. He smiled, almost laughing as he thought how she had no idea what was coming in only a couple of days, a plan he'd crafted over many months finally coming to fruition.

He reached his destination. He stood outside the shop looking in, his hand rested on the door handle, savouring the moment. It was the day that he was making the final payment on the ring. He knew he couldn't give her what she deserved but he was going to make sure that ring would be a ring that was worthy to be placed on her finger, he had refused to settle for anything less than perfect. It had felt like a lifetime, visiting that quaint little shop each week to make deposits, occasionally holding it in his hand, dreaming of that moment and also the moment he would be holding it out for her, asking her to become his wife.

He handed over the money in his hand to the old man behind the counter, in return being handed the little green velvet box. He opened it and stared at the ring sitting elegantly nestled within white satin. He thought how that ring had been worth the wait, he just had to make the proposal as exquisite.

"It's all yours now lad, when are you popping the question?" The cashier asked breaking Rob's thoughts.

"Erm, in a couple of days" He answered nodding feeling excited and nervous at the same time.

"Good luck!" the cashier replied sincerely.

"I'll need it!" he replied as he closed the box and placed it in his pocket before walking out of the shop, stepping out onto the cobbles of the old village, the village where they had spent their first date just over 12 months earlier.

He stood triumphant. He only had to wait 2 more days for his plans to reach fruition. He had thought of waiting till Valentines, but he knew the prices would be higher, and didn't want the proposal to be overshadowed by a national holiday.

As he walked back to her flat, he pondered his plans which were beginning to fall into place. He had surprised Frankie the day before with the announcement that he had booked a weekend trip to the lakes, to Lake Windermere for that coming weekend... They had been away on trips so many times that he knew she wouldn't be suspicious.

As he packed in preparation, he held the ring in is hand. He thought how they had managed to get that far, how they had enough love to see them through. He thought how with her by his side all the anguish of the past melted like snowballs in the warm sun. With her there was no worries, there was never a bar constantly out of his reach, even his lack of money did not matter.

After all that had occurred, he felt hope. It felt as though someone had stepped into this arena as his champion, someone to feel the joy of life with, and someone to ride alongside him in life. Now he had found her, he didn't want anything else. She was the one who understood him so well. He thought how his mornings started with her, his evenings ended with her. She was all he wanted and all he ever needed, he found on the rare days without her life felt wrong, craving that amazing company she gave him. In short, he worshiped her.

He thought how there was passion, and to a depth in which he never thought possible in his wildest of dreams but even those dreams had nothing in comparison. He'd found not only a partner, a lover but a best friend.

He thought how most other relationships would have cracked under such pressure. The pressure of family, of Raquel and her constant mind games and blackmail, the vicious attacks and attempts of sabotage. All of that but then also his own mind, his own health, and his failures... but for them it was as though they fortified their relationship creating a love which could never be broken.

The weekend arrived. He had booked them into a little cottage B&B. Rob packed their luggage in the car, climbing into the driver's seat, heading west out of Newcastle and out into the Lake District, each mile taking him closer to that moment he had planned with precision, a moment which had played in his mind for months.

They arrived at the quaint B&B. They entered, being guided to their room. The room was perfect. An old style four poster bed adorned with white satin sheets, the window overlooking the lake. Fresh lavender hung above the old fireplace which once would have hosted a real open fire but now was no more than an ornamental feature. As they unpacked Rob announced that they were going for a walk to enjoy the day, and that he had paid for the hotel to provide a picnic for them. The sun was shining brightly in the pre-spring atmosphere which had brought relieve. He could plan everything but the weather!

As they stood in the cosy foyer awaiting the picnic, Rob began to feel nervous, wondering if he could pull it off, whether it would go to plan, the way he had played it so many times in his mind. He wanted that weekend to be perfect in every way.

"Er, I've just got to nip back up to the room... Forgot something... wait here, I'll just be a few moments" he spoke reassuringly pecking her upon the cheek.

He stood in the room after completing the final little details ready for their return. His hand instinctively reached into his pocket to check the ring box was still there.

"Well.. Here goes!" he declared under his breath as he closed the door and skipped back down the stairs.

They walked along the country paths till they were stood upon one of the many hills overlooking the lake and the vast countryside. It was a perfect afternoon, the wind was calm, and the fog was nestled against the hillside below. The rolling green hills gave way to the broad expanse of the lake.

He had brought her up there under the guise of enjoying a picnic dinner and some quiet time together. Little did she know that there was so much more planned! They sat down upon a blanket and he encouraged her to explore the contents of the picnic basket.

The picnic was more delightful than Frankie could have imagined. A picnic basket filled with food including a cheese board and an assortment of cooked meat, crackers, rustic homemade bread, chocolate covered strawberries. In the basket along with juice was a bottle of champagne, the type which opened with a cork.

They sat eating, she smiled as he fed her the strawberries before popping the cork on the champagne, the bubbles streamed from the bottle. He poured her a glass handing it to her before filling his.

"To us!" he exclaimed allowing their glasses to clink together as a toast.

He stood up walking a few steps to the overhang looking out over the lake, the sun was slowly falling creating the most beautiful colours upon the water.

Frankie stood up and walked towards him, standing beside him, taking hold of his hand.

"It's beautiful" she stated.

"Not as beautiful as you" he replied slowly falling down onto one knee.

Frankie stood unaware as she looked out over the expanse, she turned to look at him, but he wasn't in her eyesight. She looked down to see him beside her on one knee producing a small green box.

As he opened the box her eyes fell upon the most beautiful ring, white gold with a large emerald surrounded by diamonds. Emeralds had always been her favourite stone. She stared at the stone speechless as the virescent glow reflected in her emerald eyes.

"Will you marry me?" he asked though she was already nodding before the words escaped.

"Yes! Yes! Yes!" she exclaimed beaming.

As he placed the ring on her finger, she thought how he must have used all of the money he had, and must have been saving for a while, she would have been happy with anything.

To her, it wasn't about the ring or the little details, though they were beautiful, it was seeing that to him she was the one he wanted forever, the one he'd risk his pride for, the courage to ask. That she was worth asking, but above all to know he was able to find the belief that they had a future, that he had a future. A future forever together.

"She said YES!" he shouted into the vast expanse.

"I'm the luckiest guy in the world" he again exclaimed loudly for the whole world to hear.

He couldn't stop smiling, to him it was better than winning the lottery, he'd won the girl of his dreams and he couldn't wait till the day she became his wife.

She felt like the luckiest girl in the world.

They spent the day lost in each other. Soon the sun was threatening to dip behind the horizon, cascading a puritanical bombardment of colours that were flung over the sky.

The receding blue and oranges battled the blackness. The almost receding sun shone on the lake below shining upon its deep depths, giving a radiant glow as though the final encore before bowing out below the horizon. It was as though the scene played out for only them to celebrate their union.

They headed back to the B&B, though Frankie was unaware that there was more to come. As Frankie entered their room her eyes were drawn to a bottle of wine which stood upon the dressing table, before allowing her eyes to fall upon the four-poster bed which was now adorned with red petals. A dress was hanging upon the wardrobe door.

"I've booked us a table at a local restaurant. The bottle is for after..." he indicated, winking while trying to control his cheeky grin.

As Frankie got dressed Rob was concealing his fretting that the dress wouldn't fit, that he'd got the wrong size, or just that he'd chosen wrongly. Always feeling as though he was never good enough and constantly pinching himself that this amazing woman chose him, even moreso that she said yes.

He was always waiting for the day her eyes would open and see him for what he was and find someone she deserved.

Frankie stood in the small bathroom facing the mirror staring at her reflection, her hands mirrored her figure within the dress. It felt perfect and she was more blown away by the fact that he'd thought of every detail. In the mirror she could see him sat upon the bed, his head lowered.

As she looked upon his reflection in the mirror she knew what his thoughts would be. She wondered if she could ever undo all the damage which caused him to live with such low self-esteem and self-belief.

She began fidgeting, adjusting the strap of her dress and applying another coat to her already red lips. She turned and walked towards him taking hold of his hand, he lifted his head allowing his eyes to fall upon the beauty in front of him.

"Wow!" he whispered under his breath.

"I love the dress... It is perfect! Just like you! I can't believe you thought of everything!" She replied spinning around feeling like the luckiest girl in the world.

She stopped spinning, falling into his arms. She looked up at him, at those eyes. It felt as though every ounce of air had exited her body, that touch like a magnet pulling them closer.
They could be poles apart, at opposite ends of the earth and she would still feel pulled toward him. As though each half loving the other so fully that a life alone would be meaningless.

His hand gently glided through her hair, looking at her in the same way he looked at her that first night, a look that only deepened over time. The attraction running deep into his core.

"Should we go eat?" she asked looking away knowing if she continued to gaze into those eyes that the chemistry would take over.

"I think we've got enough time to be fashionably late" he said smiling, his hand hovering just above her shoulder, just above the strap which lay perfectly upon her shoulder, and in that split second before his touch, every nerve in her body and brain was electrified with the anticipation of being together in a way that was more than words, creating an intimacy like never before. As though physically cementing that promise of the union to come.

They walked into the restaurant, waiting patiently. It looked and felt like one of those restaurants where you needed to book well in advance, not the kind of place you get a table on impulse. Her eyes were drawn to the crystal vases on each table encapsulating flowers, the low lighting which allowed the candles to provide an ambience, and delicate live piano music filled the air. Frankie stood, feeling a little flustered but as though on top of the world.

As they waited Frankie scanned the restaurant noticing that it was quite full. She looked around at the busy tables. An old couple eating side by side, one glass of wine each, studiously bent over their meals. She wondered if one day they would be that old couple... Her eyes continued to scan across to a family and their teenage children. Her eyes followed the sound of laughter to a group of young women in their thirties collapsing with helpless giggles as a stern woman dining alone nearby looked on frowning, making it obvious that she objected.

A waiter guided them to their table, a table nestled in the corner giving a level of intimacy away from the rest of the customers.

Frankie sat opposite Rob, frequently staring down at her hand, at the ring which sat perfectly upon her finger. A few moments passed.

The waiter returned with a menu, "Just a glass of house white for now, thank you." Rob commanded with confidence.

As she glanced down at the menu, she let herself soak in the ambient music for a few moments as her mind happily replayed the moments of that day.

She felt happiness like never before.

The meal was the perfect end to the perfect day. They returned back to the B&B, closing the door behind them, closing themselves away from the world, to continue where they had left off before leaving….

They spent the rest of the weekend together celebrating their engagement.

Every morning the only wake-up call was a chorus of birds that filled the trees outside while wrapped together in the soft sheets. Waking to the welcoming smell of the food cooking, and the aroma of freshly ground coffee in the kitchen below slowly making its way upwards as though inviting them.

Frankie felt blessed as she stared down at the beautiful ring which sat delicately upon her finger, everything was perfect, life was perfect, though it wasn't the room, the bed, the breakfast, or any of those little details which he had obviously painstakingly planned. It was the hugs and being close to him.

To her they could be anywhere, and she would still feel the same, it was his love, his comforting arms which encompassed her making her feel safe, arms in which she could stay forever, those eyes which spoke of a protective care providing a safe haven, eyes that she could rest in forever, and lips that she wanted to kiss forever.

He was filled with a strong sense of love that kept him going. They filled the weekend with adventure, though also spending time in their room, alone, not needing the outside world.

The weekend ended and too soon it was time for them to head home to face the world. Her family were over the moon at having him officially join the family.

Rob knew they had to tell his mother but hoped that the engagement would warm her to Frankie. His hopes were dashed, the news created friction as his mother argued with him making unreasonable demands. He knew it would only get worse once Raquel found out.

They returned to Frankie's apartment, although it had by then become his home, He still had his flat though he'd very rarely been there since they met.

He'd only kept the flat for the purpose of gaining access to Katrina. He thought about giving up the keys so many times as it just felt like a waste. He felt as though he belonged there with her.

As they entered the apartment Rob collapsed onto the settee holding his head in his hands.

"I'm so sorry.. This is impossible... it shouldn't be like this, it should be this hard, all I want to do is marry the woman I love...."

His words tore at her heart.

"Then let's make it just about us!" she exclaimed falling to her knees in front of him, her hands resting upon his knees before reaching up and mirroring his hands.

"Let's elope... Somewhere hot, like the Caribbean..." she continued.

"You know I can't afford to give you that" he replied sounding broken.

"Hey.. I'll pay, as long as we're together that's all that matters, I don't need money and expensive gifts I just need you just the way you are"

Over that past year his health had begun to take a downward turn, he struggled to work and no matter how much Frankie tried to stop him and to tell him he didn't need him to, he wanted to provide.

He'd always been brought up to believe that the man is to provide, he thought of his father and how he'd always looked up to him and imagined being like him.

His stubbornness never faltered, not wanting to feel like a failure.

Frankie watched constantly worrying wishing he would let her provide, to forget the stereotypical beliefs which his family had doctrined into him.

Chapter 12

He sat with his phone in his hand a few weeks later reading a message from Imogen. Her and Marcus were visiting her father that weekend and asked whether he wanted to meet up with them.

He thought how Frankie had never met Imogen, and although he mentioned Imogen to her, he'd glossed over their friendship, he couldn't break the confidences of a friend and explain that they'd became so close, unable to define the relationship they had built over so many years, not knowing how to put into words how he had always felt as though he had to save her, wondering if she would understand, or risking the conversation leading to opening the box of secrets of Imogen's life that he'd sworn to keep.

He wondered if he could allow them to meet, to him Imogen would always have a special place in his heart, but his heart now belonged completely to Frankie.

He met up with Imogen and Marcus that Friday down the bay as they waited for her father Brian to arrive. He'd filled her in by text that he'd proposed but hadn't gotten round to telling her how they were considering eloping, he wanted to tell her in person worried of her reaction.

Before Marcus and Frankie they'd dreamed of their weddings, of her wedding and his wedding, though back then he never believed that those days would come.

But they promised that if they were to find someone who could love them, that the other would be a part of the wedding party, they had also always promised that no matter what they would always be in each other's lives because they had a friendship like non other, that they'd pulled each other out of their darkest moments creating a bond that was unbreakable, though distance and circumstance was making even that promise hard to maintain.

When Imogen married Marcus, she kept her end of the deal, he was usher and felt like a part of the day. He knew she expected the same though he hoped she would understand. That she knew his mother, and that she would understand what levels of hell Raquel could descend too.

"So, wedding plans? Where you up to mate" Marcus asked, his time in London was evident in his changed accent.

"Erm.. well I was going to update you on that one...." Rob answered looking at Imogen, taking in a deep breath he crossed his fingers.

"With the hell that Mama and Raquel have been causing we're looking at eloping to the Caribbean..." he continued.

Imogen's face drained of all colour as she tried to hold back the tide of tears which threatened to escape.

"Sounds cool mate… Good Idea… You don't want them ruining your special day, you only marry once right…" Marcus continued nudging Imogen's shoulder.

Imogen stood up wiping her eye, looking directly at Rob before walking out.

"Leave her mate she'll be back in a few… She's been under a lot of pressure lately…" Marcus commented as he looked out of the window, his eyes following Imogen as she crossed over the road before standing holding onto the railings overlooking the bay.

"No… I know what the problem is… I better go and try and sort it.." he replied before standing up taking a drink, sighing before following her out.

He saw her standing on the other side of the road holding onto the railings, looking out over the bay watching the waves crash over the piers.

"Hey! Remember when we used to dodge those waves and sometimes end up like drowned rats?" Rob asked as he stood behind her, before stepping forward until he was standing beside her, his hands resting on the railings just a few centimetres from hers.

"It's not exactly the right time for reminiscing now is it!" she answered through the tears.

"Is that all we now amount too? Memories of when we were kids, the rose-tinted stories we'll tell our children..."

She remained rooted to the spot; the breeze was moving her hair softly away from her cheekbones. Her features buckled just slightly before she spoke, the only betrayal of her grief.

"I just want to know what happened to all the promises we made, when you said we'd always be in each other's lives, that I'd always have you, we'd always have us... I honoured those promises! From day 1 Marcus knew how much you meant to me and that he'd have to accept you as being a part of my life because you were family, you were the only real family I had, and now what...... What am I to you now?" she cried choking on her tears.

"Hey.." Rob replied as hie allowed his hand to gently rested upon hers.

Imogen moved her hand away breaking contact.

"We promised we'd be a big part of each other's wedding's but that's another broken promise... but I guess I shouldn't have expected anything else... I bet you haven't even told her about me, about us, you won't even let me meet her!"

Her thoughts began to tumble in her mind. She remembered all the scenarios she had created in her mind over the years, and that night before he met Frankie. The team she imagined they would be.

She began believing she was the problem. That the one person who always saw the good in her, making her believe she was someone, that she was worthy, was now ashamed of her. That had to be the reason. She knew deep down she was being selfish but no matter how hard she tried to fight; she couldn't fight against her emotions.

She began spiralling, her mind creating narratives that their whole friendship was all a lie. It was as though someone had pulled out a thread which held the fabric of her life together.

The heartbreak felt like a hurricane building from within. The devastation was absolute, her emotional home levelled, torn apart.

He could read her thoughts. He'd been there so many times having to ground her, to make her realise the narratives in her mind weren't real. He was always able to bring her back, as though to press reset, but this time maybe it was not going to be possible.

"Look, I meant every word and you will meet her at some point, and she does know about you, do you honestly think after everything we've been through, I'd cut you out like that. I thought you knew me better than anyone!"

"You know actions speak louder than words" she uttered, almost chocking upon the words falling from her mouth.

Wiping her eyes, she took a step back, looking over her shoulder seeing her father walking along the path towards the bay.

"Well guess we best go and keep up appearances" Imogen stated before turning to cross the road.

Rob stood there for a few moments longer thinking how selfish she was being, wondering how and why she failed to understand his point of view, that it was his life, his wedding, and his turn to have the happy ending. The happy ending that she claimed she always wanted for him, though apparently that happy ending had to be on her terms.

Pursing his lips, he thought how in a way she was right, and that maybe if he'd allowed them to meet, she wouldn't have reacted so badly. That she wouldn't be so broken-hearted.

Rob re-entered the bar. Brian turned looking up at him.

"Hi kidda, I was just gannin to the bar, want one?" Brian asked unaware of the atmosphere.

"Aye thanks Bri" Rob answered re-taking his seat.

"Have you two sorted your spat" Marcus asked, Imogen nodded in reply still trying to avoid eye-contact.

"So when are we meeting your lass?" Marcus continued finishing the last of his pint.

"Soon mate I promise..." Rob replied trying to catch Imogen's eyes.

"Maybe you could bring her down our way and we can have a night out in good old London town" Marcus continued, his sentence disturbed by Brian placing the drinks on the table and sitting next to Rob.

"So what's been gannin on..." Brian asked.

"Not seen you around for ages kidda" he continued directed at Rob.

"That's because he's got himself a woman, and got himself engaged, and planning on swanning off... Eloping to the Caribbean, but she's too good to meet the likes of us!" Imogen answered not giving Rob a chance to speak.

"Stop getting' ya knickers in a twist... You're sounding like a spoilt brat!" her father spoke sternly to Imogen.

"Congrats Kidda, if anyone deserves happiness it's you, just hope she's a good 'en, not like her mother!" Brian continued with his eyes glancing over at Imogen.

Imogen remained silent through feigned smiles trying to pretend everything was OK but inside it was destroying her.

"I could do with some work if you know of any??... To help pay for the wedding... Frankie said she'd pay but as a man I need to contribute..." Rob spoke directing his question to Brian, knowing he'd understand his need to help pay towards it.

"I'll ask around and see if I can get something sorted for Yeh' kidda"

"Thanks Bri" Rob replied.

Imogen sat feeling more and more excluded, her father didn't ask or didn't seem to care about her work, and her best friend had tossed her aside as though she was nothing.

"You could be happier for him and at least show some support for him. Thought you two were supposed to be tight" Her father stated when Rob left to go to the toilets.

"We are" Imogen answered knowing he wouldn't understand, he'd just laugh at her as though she was a pathetic kid.

She began wondering if she was being unreasonable, everyone else believed she was. When he returned, she tried to make a conceited effort, to try and appear that everything was ok.

As they left Rob stepped in giving her an embrace as though to say everything was OK, and that nothing had changed but to her it had and would never be the same again.

"Hopefully see you soon down our neck of the woods mate" Marcus spoke taking hold of Robs hand before pulling him in for an embrace.

A week past, Imogen's father had managed to get Rob some labouring work. His first day he bathed his ulcers which were beginning to cover his lower abdomen, a symptom of his kidneys which were getting progressively worse.

"I told you don't have to do this!" Frankie spoke filled with concern watching him wince with the pain.

"Please..." she begged as he kissed her.

"I got too, they're counting on me, I can't let them down" he whispered in her ear as his fingers gently touched her cheekbones scooping her hair behind her ear like he'd done so many times before.

He struggled through the day at times avoiding collapsing, that night he fell through the door into Frankie's arms.

He rang Brian to apologise, he seemed disappointed, but Rob felt that he understood.

A few days later Imogen found out he'd walked out of the job her father had arranged for her. She was still hurt and broken, and this gave an excuse to lash out, as though to kick and scream the way she'd wanted to back at the Bay.

Although it was only an excuse to lash out, to Rob it felt like a betrayal, the ultimate betrayal from one of the most important people in his life. She tore into him not realising how ill he'd been, he never told her that he was getting worse, but he thought how she shouldn't have needed to be told.

In that moment her hurt and betrayal made her see the world through blinkered eyes, not seeing the full picture. The call ended with both feeling angry and betrayed. Rob sat on his bed, his phone in his hand as the tears began to stream down his face.

He thought back over everything they had been through, the times he saved her, back when he thought nothing could break their friendship.

The betrayal, and the grief which came from it felt like a shard of glass piercing his guts. She had become family. Maybe that was why it hurt so much. He had walked with her through every storm, but she had broken him, literally into pieces.

He wiped the tears from his eyes refusing to allow it to ruin his life, his happiness. Out of all the betrayals, that one cut the deepest as though piercing his heart, as a though a small part of his heart which was where he kept her, was torn from him.

It was as though their whole relationship was shattered; where there once was love, was now consumed by an emptiness. It felt as though everyone had turned their backs on him, he could cope without them.

But to lose Imogen?

He couldn't understand how their love, their friendship, their bond which he had always believed was unbreakable, had shattered into a million pieces, how her love could turn so quickly into contempt, as if she was unwilling to fight.

She had said she loved him, that they were soulmates, twins, the one he loved like a sister, a part of each other. Over those years she had become part of the bedrock of his personality.

Those moments since he ended the call it was as though he was frozen, in shock, but as the shock began to subside his emotions took over. Emotional pain flowed out of his every pore. From his mouth came a cry so raw.

He grabbed onto a chair so that his violent shaking would not cause him to fall and from his eyes came a thicker flow of tears than he had ever cried before, moreso than even after the betrayals by his mother and siblings. He expected it from his family, but not from her.

The pain was almost enough to break him. Had it not been for Frankie that betrayal would have killed him. He fell to his knees, falling into the arms of Frankie. He continued to cry as though his brain was being shredded from the inside, as though grieving, as though in bereavement, in a way that was true because the Imogen he had known was no longer.

As he continued to cry in Frankie's arms his mind continued to overanalyse what had occurred, as though trying to make sense of such a loss.

Did she care? Did he ever mean anything to her? Or was he just a crutch she used. He tried to fight to remember the good memories, to find a way to understand. His thoughts began to tumble through his mind. Maybe he was in part to blame? Maybe she was right?

He tried to recall when they would laugh together, to try and hold on to the sweet memories of who they were, but the grief was too vast. It continually felt as though a knife was piercing his chest, though the person holding the knife wasn't an enemy but instead his closest friend, though any resemblance to that old friend was just the outer shell.

His friend was gone.

He paced the room as his grief turned into anger, becoming resolute to not think of her again. If she wanted to salvage their relationship, she would have to make the first move, he wasn't going to allow her to dampen his happiness, for once he was putting himself first.

He thought how now it was just him and Frankie, and he was Ok with that. He didn't need anyone else as long as he had her.

He always expected Imogen to ring or text, to apologise, to beg forgiveness... But as the weeks past he knew she wasn't going to, like him she was waiting, both expecting the other to make the first move.

As the weeks rolled into a month, then 2 months he shrugged his shoulders and accepted their friendship was over. He was too excited planning their wedding to let it upset him, he had the world, he had the most perfect woman in the world. But still, every now and then when a picture caught his eye, or a memory played on his mind he was overcome with a moment of sadness, a moment of grief, before taking a deep breath, allowing the moment to pass as though expelling her with his exhaled breath,

He packed up all of the pictures of them, all the letters, the poems, the scribbled notes, anything that would remind him of a friendship lost, as though to be able to forget her and the life they'd made together all those years, to try and limit the memories.

He stood over the outside bin, the box in his hands, though couldn't bring himself to let go, instead he stepped back, walking to the small shed where Buzby sat. He threw he box into the corner thinking how one day he may be able to look at them again, but until then they were out of sight, just like she was out of mind.

Rob and Frankie arranged to get married in Jamaica later that year.

It felt as though time had slowed down as they began to countdown the days.

Chapter 13

Those following months were a rollercoaster as they eagerly awaited their upcoming wedding. They had many weekends spent with Katrina, as though they were a family. The family he always dreamed of.

One summer's day they sat upon the golden sand at Cullercoats bay. The waves lapped upon the sand as Frankie lovingly watched Rob and Katrina play.

She watched as they rolled around in the sand, watching as he lifted her high in the air as she giggled with delight. Katrina was now a toddler. She watched as she ran across the sand on unsteady feet to reach the arms of her loving father. Wobbling to and fro, before falling on her bottom, then clapping like it was all part of the plan and rolled to her stomach to get up again, taking a few steps while giggling, waving her arms for the pick-up she knew was coming, again being hoisted high. She watched the smile upon Rob's face, a smile which could light up the whole town.

She also observed how as they played Rob fell to the ground allowing Katrina to climb upon him, to beat him up, and Rob was all too willing to play along.

He doubled himself up and burst into a loud chortle of laughter. As she climbed upon him, his fingers began to wiggle with a mischievous smile playing upon his lips.

His fingers found their way to her tickling spots causing an outburst of that laughter he loved. Taking hold of her he stood up and spun her round in the air until he felt dizzy. He was in that state of intoxication. They fell on to the soft sand wriggling with laughter.

Rob sat back down.

"Your turn.." he stated.

He sat content with his hands behind his head as he watched them. He caught Katrina's beaming smile. Her smile so beautiful, he knew that one day she would be breaking hearts. He listened to Katrina's sweet laughter, laughing so delicately.

Her laughter was like ripples upon a still pond after a stone has been thrown in. It radiated outwards. A sound that every time Rob heard it, no matter how he was feeling, it brightened his day. But when combined with the laughter of Frankie, made his world brighter. It was a laughter that Rob could feel deep in his lungs, so deep that it took his breath away.

Whenever he heard her laughter or even just looked upon that caring face, he felt blessed, she provided a constant relief from all the distress that shoved its way into his brain.

Both laughter's combined it felt as though everything in life was perfect, as though the sounds of their laughter lifted a veil allowing him to see the world more clearly, reaching deep into the depths of his soul.

Those precious weekends as a family were sporadic. There were periods of time when the contact was every weekend, but Rob knew that it didn't take much to set Raquel off, times when she would react and remove contact as a way of punishing him. It was as though it was her way of keeping some control, as though she got satisfaction from it...

Some days the weight of the manipulation was almost enough to break him, especially when she teamed up with his family, but the memories from those precious weekends kept him going and kept him fighting, he knew what was at stake. He would fight for that little girl to the end of his days, and he was never going to let any of them destroy the perfect love that he had found.

That summer he finally handed back the keys to his flat, moving in officially with Frankie, to begin planning their new future together, both eagerly looking forwards to their wedding.

Through that summer, on some days when Frankie was at work, he sat in his parent's garage tinkering with Buzby. The downside of giving up his flat meant losing his small shed which had been more like a garage, a home for Buzby. Grudgingly his mother allowed him to keep Buzby and some of the contents of his old shed and his tools there.

His rides had become few and far between as at first, as she brought back too many memories of a friendship broken, but then as he began to feel able to face being around the bike, he began to find riding difficult. He was beginning to develop abscesses, and began suffering intermittent abdominal pain, which was intensified by the riding position. Both side effects of his failing kidneys. Also, Buzby was beginning to fall apart, she was getting old, too old... And all his money was being saved for his new dream, his new love. Frankie... And their dream wedding.

One ride she finally gave up. He was returning from a ride along the coast up to Amble and back. A route he had taken on Buzby so many times over the years. Returning along those old country roads he was cruising at 50mph when she began to lose speed, spluttering. He managed to keep riding though barely managing to push her over 30mph, eventually she gave up, cutting out as he neared the bay. He tried kickstarting to no avail, in the end having to push her the final mile back to his Mother's house.

He knew it was going to take a lot of work to get her fixed.

"One day girl we'll get you back on the road... One day...." He whispered before closing the garage door.

Chapter 14

October.

The day had finally arrived for them to set off for their wedding.

Excitement filled the air. Rob and Frankie had started their journey to London to stay at Gatwick over night before commencing their wedding journey to Jamaica, to the Sandles resort.

The journey down from Newcastle had been long. They stepped into the hotel lobby at Gatwick airport. The polished lobby desk was made of cherry-wood. Warm smells of home-cooking wafted through the warm air. The cosy atmosphere was a welcome change from the cramped train, but even that hadn't been enough to kill their mood. They were one step closer.

They were ushered to their room. Placing the bags on the floor Rob fell backwards upon the soft bed, his arms outstretched.

As dusk began to fall they walked back down to the lobby to the restaurant within the hotel. The restaurant was bustling with others like them using the hotel as a pitstop in their journey to their holiday destinations, businessmen and women in their suits, and tourists, trying to decipher the menu.

They enjoyed an amazing dinner in the hotel talking about their pending wedding and how amazing they both felt. Rob continued to pinch himself. He had waited for this moment for so long, but always thought it would never arrive, something would go wrong, something always went wrong. Now his dream was in touching distance. One final sleep, that following day they were flying out to Jamaica, and that 2 days after they were getting married.

Morning came. The sun poured through their windows as the sound of the alarm clock began to slowly increase in volume. Rob and Frankie jumped out of the bed, excitedly getting ready before fastening their bags, taking one final check that they had everything before making their way to the lobby for the shuttlebus to the airport a few moments away...

They arrived at the airport where they were booked into the first-class lounge. Happiness and love were all they felt, fuelled by pure excitement.

The lounge was quiet which provided a relief from the bustle in the rest of the airport. They sat down with their drinks looking out of the window at the runway below, watching planes taxiing to the terminal. Another couple entered the lounge. As always Rob's infectious nature welcomed them. The couple sat on the adjacent table and soon they were talking as though they had known each other forever.

They discovered the couple, Clive and Ava, were also going to the same hotel. Frankie was bemused, wondering what the chances were of meeting two people who were going to the same place. Out of all the destinations in the world, and all the hotels...

They entered the plane, walking up the stairs to the first-class seating. Rob sat down, his hands gripping the arm rests finding the seats to be amazingly comfortable. He was very tall, taller than others who were labelled as tall. He had flown back and forward to Spain and Gram Canaria throughout his life but from his mid-teens he found himself cramped into the small seats with very little leg room. In first class he had room to stretch out.

On the plane they found that they were in adjacent seats to Clive and Ava.

The plane moved slowly before gaining speed and altitude. As the plane steadied in the air the stewardess walked down the aisle.

"More Champagne Sir?" She asked holding a bottle.

"Why not! Drinks all round!" he answered beaming, inviting their new friends to join them.

The Champagne started to flow, inviting Clive and Ava to join them in toasting to their impending wedding.

"I've always wanted to attend a wedding at Sandals" Ava commented.

"Come to ours!" Rob exclaimed without any thought or hesitation.

The conversations carried on throughout the long flight.

The easy-going camaraderie ignited the kind of friendship that they all knew would carry on through their lives.

By the end of the flight it had been decided that Clive and Ava were not only going to attend their wedding but to become witnesses.

The flight took over 10 hours, by the time they arrived they were both tired yet at the same time were both still wired with excitement.

The plane landed. As they stepped off the plane the heat hit them. They climbed down the stairs onto the runway. They walked through the airport, their bags had been collected by staff and placed into a car. A car which was waiting for them to take them to the resort.

They felt like VIP's, they had only just landed but it felt so magical, so beautiful, and tranquil.

They entered the hotel nestled within the resort, only a few yards from the golden beach. They stood in the foyer waiting at the reception for further instructions. The desk was made of amber-coloured wood and a burnt orange granite top. The floor of the exquisite hotel was tiled in fine marble, which made every step echo.

A chandelier caught the mid-day sun creating rainbow colours which danced across the luxurious foyer and into the adjoining lobby.

The twin doors that led into the lobby were a pristine white with golden handles. Embroidered silk sofas lay in the far corner of the lobby, with staggered positioning, though most faced the large, flat-screen television which hung upon the wall. Exquisite paintings hung from the rich, golden walls. Even the door hinges were engraved with swirls and elegant designs. The domed ceiling rose at least 100 feet high.

They were escorted to their room, with their own butler champagne awaiting them. Their room was on ground level with the sliding doors opening up to an exclusive Swimming pool. It felt as though they were royalty, an experience they wanted to never end, an experience never to forget.

The remainder of the day was spent relaxing, an afternoon swim taking in the sun on the lounge chairs, aiming to get a little tan before their big day, and meeting up with Clive and Ava before dinner.

The following day following breakfast they sat waiting in a small room set aside from the main lobby for a meeting with the wedding team to discuss the final arrangements for the wedding the following day. They sat hand in hand, the excitement was overwhelming.

The night before the wedding a reservation had been made for them to eat at a French restaurant within the resort. Rob was excited to try the caviar, feeling like a king! The caviar cost more than what he would earn in a month, but it was all included in the package, so for those few days he was going to live the life he knew his future bride deserved. They gazed into each other's eyes as the waiter poured their wine, both lost in each other and the knowledge that that time the next day they would be husband and wife.

Rob stood up with his glass in his hand.

"You are all invited tomorrow to watch me marry the most beautiful woman in the entire world!" he exclaimed.

Frankie watched her husband to be, watching him come alive with a confidence she had only seen glimpses of. As she watched him, she reflected on how she had never heard him so happy, so full of life, overflowing with the excitement of the upcoming wedding all over his face. It was as though he was intoxicated, but not by alcohol but instead intoxicated from her love.

What made the experience even more amazing was that there was no-one there to spoil it, no one who knew their history, his history, no one to bring him down, to make him feel un-worthy.

All people saw was a perfect couple madly in love, a couple perfect for each other who were about to cement that love in a union that no one could break.

Rob pulled her to her feet kissing her. She stared into his eyes as the restaurant erupted in applause. The love in Rob and Frankie's eye shone for everyone to see.

Following dinner, they took a walk along the cool sands watching the sun set on the eve of their wedding before heading back to their room, closing the door behind them.

Chapter 15

The big day arrived. Frankie awoke to sunshine pouring through the balcony windows, birds singing outside, and butterflies doing circus tricks in her stomach. Frankie stood in the hotel room staring at her reflection in the mirror. She thought how that day her life was going to change. Every moment from the day they met had brought them to that day. They had triumphed and overcame all the odds, even when it felt as though the whole world was against them.

Frankie was escorted to the salon to get her hair and make-up done. She entered the salon which had been closed for her exclusive use. She sat in the white leather chair facing the mirror, with her new friend Ava in the seat next to her. Music filled the air as a tall woman popped the cork on a bottle of sparkling wine before filling crystal glasses. They both sat in complete relaxation as they were handed the glasses while a team of staff worked on their hair and make-up for the ceremony. Although she had only known Ava for a short time it felt so special to share that special experience with her.

Rob stood feeling lost, beginning to panic, wondering what if something was to go wrong... His thoughts were disturbed by a knock at the door. He answered it, finding Clive standing in the doorway holding a bottle of whiskey.

"Come on, no time for dithering... We've got a wedding to get ready for" he winked as he entered the room.

"Which one is mine?" he asked looking at the suits in white suit bags hanging on the door of the wardrobe.

"First though... Drinks!" he exclaimed pouring the whiskey into two tumblers.

Rob sat swirling the whiskey in his glass. He couldn't believe that day had arrived, he felt as though he had to pinch himself to prove it wasn't a dream. He remembered the day that time stood still, the day he proposed. Kneeling, breath held until the sound of that soulful yes, he remembered the feeling of joy, and how that joy blossomed every moment onwards, bringing them to this moment.

In the weeks and months leading up to that day, since that proposal, he'd daydreamed about the promises they were going to make and the vows that they would commit to. He was so excited to become Frankie's husband, and have her to become his wife. Many just saw it as a piece of paper but to Rob it meant so much more, it wasn't just a ring worn, or a contract signed. It was something to be savoured. Marriage was the union of two hearts beating as one. It was proclaiming to God, and to the world that they had won out against all, that they were unbreakable.

Once the hair and make-up were complete, they were escorted to a room, where her bouquet lay elegantly upon the table, Wild posies of native flowers, sweet-peas, greenery and fragrant herbs of which the scent filled the air, the sort of refreshing scent which was perfect to carry on a hot day.

Their dresses were hanging, hidden inside white satin suit bags. She had chosen the style and given her sizes but this was the first time she would set eyes upon the dress itself. Nervously yet also excited she slowly unzipped the bag. The dress being revealed for all to see.

Her wedding dress could have been made for royalty. A dream-dress for a dream-day with her own Prince Charming.

She was laced into her dress before turning to see her reflection in the mirror, taking in the extravagant lace and light satin which was perfect for such a tropical wedding.

She stood in awe seeing her reflection staring back, it was hard for her to believe that was her and not an illusion through the looking glass. Her dress was simple but perfect. It looked as though it was designed just for her.

The A-line silhouette of the dress accentuated her figure. Although it flared out at the waist it was subtle, not like the ballgown style of dress which was almost synonymous to a bride.

The neckline managed to blend together a bateau style made out of lace with a jewel neckline which elongated her neck by gently following the curves of her collarbone. The lace provided a hint of sensuality, showing the right amount of flesh without taking away from the elegance..

She wanted to engrave the memories of those moments. Like all brides she was keen to fast forward to the ceremony, but she knew those memories would come to mean more in the future. A stray tear of joy escaped from her eye, the first of what she knew would be many, she hoped her make up would last through the tears.

She continued to stand gazing upon her reflection. She saw herself and could see her life up until that moment. She had always been a happy person but had never really know happiness and contentment until she met Rob.

His love had widened her eyes and views upon life. All of her experiences had affected how she saw the world, and people, but although he had a lifetime of betrayals and hurdles, and had his heart ripped from his chest on more than one occasion he was still the most selfless man you could meet.

She could never understand how he never let circumstance change him. He changed her, though at times she had to be a voice of reason to save him from giving too much of himself, some people were like wolves and would take and take and tear a good heart apart till there was nothing left.

Their differences complimented each other, many had said they were too different, but with him she realised there was truth in 'opposites attract'.

She thought of the last time she stood in a white dress, young and fresh stepping out into the unknown, unaware of what she was walking into. Her reflection this time was different. Her beauty was now accentuated with maturity with a dollop of innocence thrown in.

She felt free, she loved life and she met the love of her life. She'd never known what love was until she found Rob, he was her knight in shining armour. She reflected back on her life with him, the prelude to the life ahead of them.

She smiled as she remembered his touch in the middle of the night... She adored his little habits - hugging her in his sleep, tickling her, playing games with her, just sitting there with her in total silence, even his snoring to which he would exclaim he was dreaming that he was a motorcycle. She was filled with little memories that so often get passed over as mundane. Memories of his arms embracing her from behind as she washed dishes in the kitchen. Remembering the little moments when she'd grumble at him, whenever he did those little irritating things, then laugh as his cheeky smile which became infectious. The way they worked as a team, the way he always came to help her, never letting her carry bags, opening doors for her, the perfect gentleman making her feel like a princess. Her life had hung on his whispered sweet nothings... Having him just being near her.

She remembered all this, and she wept... Though the tears were happy tears.

There was still plenty of time before the ceremony, plenty of time to soak up the atmosphere and live in the moment, time spent dancing, singing along to old songs, chatting away, really getting to know each other and flowing into conversations about adventures of the past and dreams for the future.

The clock ticked loudly as though counting down to the moment when they needed to leave. The photographer had left to take photos of the groom before the ceremony. That moment she had dreamed of was getting closer.

15 minutes before they were due to leave was time for a quick touch up of make-up and for her tiara to be placed with great precision upon her head, and delicately pinned into place, the final touch. They had one final celebratory cheer and a few more tears as their classes clinked together one final time.

They finished their drinks. It was time to go.

They left the quaint little room and danced through the grounds of the hotel, down towards the beach where the ceremony was to take place, just above the water's edge.

Rob stood waiting patiently for Frankie to arrive...

The sky was clear blue. A crisp breeze gently rolled in off the waves which lapped the sand, bringing just enough coolness to bring comfort as he stood in his suit.

He caught glimpse of her in the distance. As soon as he saw her coming the tears started to flow. Even from that distance she was mesmerising, as though having the power to emit a hypnotic effect upon anyone who saw her.

As Frankie stepped onto the wooden walkway which led onto the beach a deep sense of serenity overcame her. She stared in rapture at the expanse of blue that lay before her. Rays of lights danced delicately across the water, birthed from the afternoon sun that both limited her sight and made the view all the more beautiful.

White pebbles created an aisle for her to walk down towards her groom. As she stepped onto the sand and allowed her eyes to follow the pebbles to the white pergola against the emerald warm waters and the waves gently lapping the sand, creating the perfect backdrop.

Slowly she began walking, she could see Rob standing by the pergola waiting patiently.

She paused for a moment, standing barefoot upon the warm white sand in her beautiful white wedding gown, wanting to savour every moment. Her dress was almost dazzling as the mid-day sun was reflected back, she had a radiance, a glowing from deep within which magnified with each step.

The simple beauty of the way the scene had been set created the perfect and private atmosphere that he had envisioned. As she approached the marquee, she passed her bouquet to Ava, taking hold of Rob's hands.   As she held his hand, she started to cry more tears of sheer happiness and joy for what was about to take place.

He looked at his bride standing by his side, he was overcome with emotion. She looked amazing, breath-taking, elegant. He had always seen her as the most beautiful woman in the world but standing there she was even more beautiful than he could ever have imagined. She emanated a peaceful assured happiness that most wait their whole lives to experience.

They began to recite their vows. It was intimate and emotional, a celebration of love, a dream come true after many obstacles.

Guests from the restaurant and some guests which they had met those past few days began to walk across the beach in their direction, closing in on the ceremony unfolding in front of them, watching Frankie and Rob declaring their love and commitment for each other. Their love which was obvious to everyone who had seen them together, but their love was especially evident in that moment.

He didn't want to say 'until death do us part,' Not starting their new life of love by thinking about death. He's spent too much of his life focussing on his death.

Death meant being torn apart from her, instead he wished he could say forever. He wanted to spend a thousand lifetimes with her.

Wanting the...

".. and they lived happily ever after."

To believe that their love was powerful enough to always be together in this life and beyond.

He continued through the vows he had written, but no words could ever say enough, they were soulmates, pure and simple, two halves that complete one another, perfectly complimenting, yet unique.

After the ceremony and the officiant had declared...

"I now pronounce you Husband and wife…. You may now kiss the bride"

The beach erupted, all of those people were on their side, were cheering for them. Cheering from people they barely knew, people they'd only just met but had become invested in their love story.

Although surrounded by people they were lost in each other, a few moments of intimacy, that first kiss as husband and wife more magical than any kiss which had come before.

Food and drinks were brought down onto the beach and placed upon tables on both side of the wedding cake and flowers as the photographer snapped photos of the couple.

After the photos they joined the guests which had culminated around them giving a champagne toast to celebrate.

They were now husband and wife.

As the food was shared Frankie stepped back, watching her husband. It was custom to throw the bouquet, but they had never been into convention and tradition, instead she placed her bouquet upon the sand and etched a large heart around it, and their initials, her new initials. She was now Mrs Reagan and was proud to take his name.

She took a moment to let that sink in and reflected on how that day was even more perfect than she had ever imagined it to be, it was truly magical, the best thing that had ever happened to them and it wasn't spoiled by anything or anyone.

Well almost.....

As the celebrations continued, Rob became slightly intoxicated as the drinks continued to flow, causing him to decide to take an impromptu jump into the sea. As he stood in the water, he declared.

"That beautiful woman is now my wife"

Frankie walked towards the water's edge, towards her husband. She took his hand to guide him out, back onto the sand, but instead he pulled her into an embrace. It wasn't long after he noticed his wedding band was missing, having fallen off in the water. Normally an incident like that would have caused him to kick himself, but nothing could ruin that day, instead he rallied the guest to enter the water to help him find his ring.

Dusk began to slowly descend upon the beach. Fireworks were timed perfectly as a festive backdrop for the newlyweds' cutting the cake.

The crowds began to disperse. A few clouds began to roll in. The golden day sun began to blend into tones akin to red-velvet as the sun slowly began to set creating a perfect sunset against the white sand as though crowning the sweetest of days. They watched as a dolphin arced out of the water in the distance as though especially for them. The day had culminated in pure bliss and perfection, it felt like heaven.

They returned to their room where the bed had been adorned with rose petals and the room filled with scented candles to create the perfect end to a perfect day. The day had ended, but the night was still young. She stood staring into those loving eyes.

"We're going to have a long and wonderful life together, I just know it.." he whispered as his hand softly brushed her cheekbone, down upon her neck and along to the straps of her dress.

His touch was warm and tender. It wasn't going to be their first time together but would be the first as husband and wife. It felt so different, like a dream. He moved in closer also feeling the anticipation of that first night. He wrapped his arms around her, kissing her softly causing her to feel weak at the knees. She turned until he was behind her. Softly he scooped her hair over her shoulder before carefully undoing the lace which allowed the dress to fall. She stood in anticipation wanting nothing more than to consummate their union. She turned facing him, he moved in closer allowing the passion that had been building since the moment he had first saw her stepping out onto the sand to explode. They made love well into the night.

The following morning, they awoke, the dawning of the first day as husband and wife. A breakfast was delivered to their room, adorned with fresh flowers, orange juice, and sparkling wine.

Rob and Frankie enjoyed the rest of their holiday as a honeymoon...

But soon the day to head home arrived, heading back home.

Chapter 16

They had only been home 2 days before Rob received a text

I hear ur home. Did ya get hitched? Hope it went without any problems, we wouldn't want that... Cause if you are now married I am going to take Frankie for everything she has!.

They had hoped for a few days before the onslaught began again. They knew she must have been told by his mother; she was the only one who knew they were back. It always felt like a dagger in his chest that his own mother would side with someone like her, that she would take her side over that of her own blood, and how she could be so oblivious to the games she played. How could his family not see through her the way everyone else did?

Rob placed the phone down, not acknowledging the message, and not wanting Frankie to see it but he could never keep anything from her.

Frankie decided that enough was enough. She had gone too far. She was going to arrange to meet her under the guise that she was meeting with Rob. In all their year's together she had never come face to face with Raquel. She assumed like all bullies she was too afraid to face someone she couldn't abuse and manipulate.

Frankie thought how she had no idea who she was dealing with or what was coming her way. But Frankie knew revenge was a dish best served cold...

They had a wedding reception to attend first.

Saturday evening, they headed down to Crusoe's. A quaint café/restaurant built upon Longsands creating the perfect beach/surf atmosphere. They had hired the restaurant and had it decorated following a Jamaican theme.

A Steel band were playing. The restaurant embellished in Jamaican colours. Family, friends, and work colleagues were invited to help celebrate their marriage. The night felt perfect, though Frankie couldn't help but feel vexed that Rob's family were acting loving and supportive, as though playing a role for the other guests. She knew they wouldn't want people to know the truth. There were times she wanted to shout it from the rooftops, but she knew how that would shatter her husband. She knew if she did, they would retaliate, throwing mud, stooping to depths that she knew Rob would never dare to tread, they would eat him alive and destroy him even more than they already had.

She watched as Rob beamed, he was in his element, even getting up and making elaborate speeches. She felt so proud. His eyeline caught his brother standing at the bar. Frankie followed his line of sight, and in that moment, she saw the smirk upon Owen's face. Rob allowed that look to knock his confidence for a moment.

Frankie wished he could see himself for who he was instead of constantly seeking their approval. She gripped his hand tightly as to transfer some of her strength to him.

Rob turned his gaze from Owen to his wife. Looking into her eyes made him feel strong enough to conquer anything. He stood silent for a moment as his thoughts meandered through his mind still wondering what he did to deserve her. He thought how every time he felt as though he'd failed, that he'd not done enough, or had allowed his mind to cause him to be irrational, to self-sabotage, when he thought she would have had enough there was only patience, freely given, never needing earned.

That was what grace was. He had never accepted grace, never feeling he deserved it, never feeling worthy, or at times feeling too proud to humble himself. He always needed to feel strong, to need to be seen as strong. He had been in need of healing. True healing though takes time. There had been no magic wands for the deep pain within. When he met her he was broken. With her love, her endless patience, time, and her inner strength she had fixed him, filling his cracks with love.

He was no longer the man they had made him into, the man they claimed he was to justify their behaviour.

He smiled as he squeezed her hand in reciprocation. Before turning back to the guests.

"Sorry for that guys and gals but I got lost in the eyes of the most beautiful woman in the world... So where was I?" he declared with confidence bursting out of him.

They partied well into the night. As the guests left, they stood in each other's arms.

They scanned the room, looking at the table in the far corner, a table filled with many wrapped gifts. They had received so many gifts they were overwhelmed beyond belief.

"Well we should somehow pack all this stuff up and head home" Rob declared.

"Yep" Frankie nodded thinking how that night marked the beginning of their future together.

The day after the wedding reception Frankie picked up Rob's phone which lay on the arm of the settee. Rob was unaware, in the bathroom running his wife a bath.

Meet me tomorrow outside the Bay

A few seconds later his phone pinged.

11am. Don't be late! I wont be hanging around waiting!

Frankie smiled as she sent a final reply.

I'll be there

Smiling she walked through the apartment and into the bathroom wrapping her arms around her husband. He turned. Standing on tiptoes she leant in kissing him.

"What was that for?"

"Do I need a reason?" she replied as her smile became mischievous.

Her hand reached down, scooping some of the bubbles from the bath, taking a step back she plastered the bubbles over his face.

"Right! This is how we're playing is it?" he replied scooping up a handful of bubbles and chasing her through the apartment into the bedroom.

Their playfight was disturbed by a crash coming from the open plan living room. They walked slowly out from the bedroom and along the short corridor, peering in. The glass dining table had exploded. Shards of glass covered the room and the furniture.

"This is going to take some cleaning... And we will need a new one. Guess it's good we weren't in here" Rob said as he scanned the room.

"Why don't we get new everything... New furniture, things that are ours that we can choose together, and maybe while we're at it a house?" Frankie replied wrapping her arms around him.

The next day...

Frankie arrived at the Bay. She stood waiting, stepping back and forth, staring down at her watch then up and down the street. The icy cold North Sea breeze was making it feel a lot colder than it was, it was so cold she could barely formulate a thought as her mind began to replay what she wanted to say, determined to put Raquel in her place and finally lay down the law.

As the minutes past Frankie began wondering if she would turn up, or that she would turn up, see her then run for the hills like the coward she was.

As Raquel saw Frankie waiting there her face sank with fear although she tried to hide it. She thought about turning and walking away, Frankie hadn't seen her yet, or had she?

She stood frozen to the spot unable to make that decision, fight or flight, but then all to late the decision was made for her as Frankie turned looking directly at her.

Frankie began walking towards her, in response Raquel also began walking keeping a poker face to hide her true emotions wearing a mask of defiance and surety.

"Right! I hear you are going to take me for everything I have now that I'm married to Rob" Frankie spoke confidently.

Raquel stood frozen in the stand-off. She tried to find some flicker of fear, that she was bluffing but Frankie was resolute, her emotions unreadable, no fear, with an intensity in her tone that spoke volumes, as though saying 'Try me'.

Frankie stood in the silence expecting a reply, one that never came.

"Well, just to let you know I have hired a solicitor. Katrina is not my child so there is NOTHING you can do.."

Frankie paused for a moment as though to give Raquel a chance to try and defend herself.

"I LOVE Katrina like my own…. But you better back off or it'll be the biggest mistake you have ever made" Frankie continued with a great deal of emotion behind the words she was speaking.

" I er, I er" Raquel began to respond.

Frankie looked at her remaining resolute.

"I didn't mean it like that.." she continued, her head down.

"Yes you did! It stops now!" Frankie answered before turning and walking away, a smile began to creep across her face feeling satisfied.

She took a glance back over her shoulder to see Raquel still standing there, lost, defeated.

Frankie began walking faster, her hands joined as though to bring warmth. She sat in her car smiling before turning the key in the ignition, pulling away, heading home.

She arrived back at their estate, parking outside of the apartment block. She exited the car looking around at the houses, brick and uniform, and gardens taking on a wintery feel, knowing soon those gardens would be adorned with Christmas lights and inflatable Santa's and snowmen. She thought how that Christmas would most likely be the last in that small flat, excited for their new beginning, their new home, their new life, their married life. She turned back towards the apartment block to see him standing in the doorway, walking towards her with that face, that smile, that look of pure love he reserved only for her, just the way she loved it - just natural, relaxed, perfect.

"Where have you been?" Rob asked inquisitively.

"Nowhere important" She replied leaning forwards on her tiptoes, kissing him.

"Come on" she continued taking his hand, walking back down the path, into the apartment block, the door closed behind them.

Chapter 17

January. A New year, a new start, a new home......

They stood in the doorway of a semi-detached house nestled in the corner of a remote cul-de-sac. Their new home. Three bedrooms, a living room, a separate lounge and a large kitchen with it's own breakfast bar. A large south facing garden. They had longed for a garden. Rob had imagined them sitting on sun loungers watching the clouds pass by as they soaked up the summer sun.

It also had a garage. It was too small for Frankie to feel comfortable parking her mini, but they knew it would be ideal for Rob to keep Buzby and all of his tools. Since moving from his flat he had to keep Buzby back at his mother's house.

Many times, his brothers had threatened to scrap it. To them it was a worthless heap of metal, unsightly and bringing down the tone of the garage, but to Rob that bike was priceless, even if it didn't run.

Also, in his mother's garage were all of his father's tools. He knew his father would have wanted him to have them, though he knew his brothers would try to prevent him taking them, not because they wanted them or had any use of them, but more so just to get one up on him, to deny him, to fuel their own amusement.

They entered the house which felt so big and bare. As Rob scanned the blank canvass in front of him, he thought how home was wherever she was, his home was in her arms.

"We'll turn it into a home" Rob declared kissing Frankie's head as his mind began to create a multitude of design ideas.

He finally had a home, somewhere that he could work on, a fresh canvass, but above all something that belonged to the both of them.

They returned to the apartment. Cardboard boxes filled the rooms, each box scrawled on in black broad felt-tip marker, to convey the contents and room for which it was intended. The walls were bare, devoid of the usual smiling framed faces, only the change in shade of the paint gave an indication of where pictures once hung. The bright toned squares against the lighter toned background showing where the sun had failed to reach.

white parcel labels were stuck on black binbags filled with clothes. There was only a few more things to pack before the removal van was to arrive.

The belongings were taken downstairs to be loaded onto the van. As each thing was packed the apartment, which was once a home, returned to an empty shell awaiting new life. They had shared so many memories in that small apartment, but there was many more to make.

After the last box was taken, they stood in what once was the living room. Dirt and dust shapes marked the floor like templates of the furniture that once stood there.

A single shard of glass twinkled as the sunlight caught it's surface, a stray shard of glass from the shattered table. Rob walked over picking it up.

"Should we keep it? A souvenir?" He questioned.

Frankie shook her head laughing in disbelief.

"What am I going to do with you.. You clown"

"I aim to please" he winked in reply.

They settled into their new home. Rob used his days to design and decorate, though some days less was completed. He was slowly finding it harder to do all the things he once did with ease. He was getting old, but he knew it was more than that. He knew his kidneys were slowly deteriorating. Although it took a few months, he had turned the house into a home, their home.

He thought of all the times he had helped others move and decorate. He'd always been there whenever anyone asked, but he was finding when the shoe was on the other foot all of those people who were constantly begging for his help vanished. Just like when he wanted to pick up Buzby, the lack of replies or offers of help were nowhere to be seen.

Instead, he decided to push the bike home, it took a long time, and he had to stop multiple times, and was glad Frankie was at work so didn't see how much he struggled, how much pain it caused, but he felt a relief, a triumph at doing it alone, not needing to rely on fair-weather friends.

He told himself he would remember the silence, though knew that if anyone asked for his help he'd still go running. They picked the tools up in Frankie's car, taking multiple trips, but eventually everything found its way to their rightful place.

Rob was at his happiest, Buzby in the garage, his tools, and all of his father's tools that he cherished so dearly, the tools he had held with his small hands as his father tried to teach him how to use them. Holding them made him feel closer to him, as though a part of his father was still there with him.

The months began to roll into each other. All to quickly Summer was on the horizon.

Frankie could see Rob was beginning to look tired. She decided it was time to have another holiday to give Rob some sun and relaxing. This time, this holiday, to Gran Canaria. Rob was excited at the thought of his extended family meeting his wife. Although there was at first some resistance, Raquel agreed to allow Katrina to join them.

That April they set off for their first 'family' holiday.

They stayed in a small villa nestled within the picturesque resort. In the distance the Rocky volcanic Mountains rose up on the horizon, the base softened by desert areas and open plains which merged into the old town which snaked its way down to the shore.

It was a place Rob had visited so many times over the years, memories of being a small boy running down the old, cobbled streets. It was the first time Frankie had been there, and the first time for Katrina. He hoped it would be the first of many, that she would grow up and be able to look back on fond memories just like he could.

They spent the days meeting family, family gatherings and meals, feeling welcomed and loved. They spent days exploring the old towns, and the vast hills, and days riding camels, They also had many days spent on the soft sandy beach building sandcastles and splashing in the warm Mediterranean Sea,

Rob sat on the beach with the soft golden sand providing just the right amount of comforting warmth, sitting with his arm draped over Frankie's shoulder as he watched Katrina playing. His eyes scanned across the sore from sand to stone, from rockpool to breaking waves. It was a time for playing, and days for dreaming, wishing they could all stay there forever.

The holiday was about being together as a family creating memories. Those 2 weeks past too quickly, the day to return home coming too fast.

Chapter 18

A year past.

April.

Spring was approaching bringing new life. Life had been perfect, even Raquel had been behaving, the threat of custody and the risk of social workers becoming involved was enough to keep her under control. Katrina was continuing to grow, starting school, coming into her own, and loving being with daddy. She was Daddy's little girl in every way. She spent almost every weekend with Rob and Frankie.

The year of peace was in reality just a ruse to catch them off guard, their defences down, still lost in the honeymoon phase. Unbeknown to them his family had been scheming with Raquel. They had been getting close to him in order to try and undermine him as a father, to prove him as unfit so that Raquel could use it against him.

Katrina's birthday an envelope landed on the doormat, an official letter listing his faults and apparent failings as a father. A letter removing access. In it he was labelled as an alcoholic. His past being dragged up, the letter claimed that his drinking problem wasn't behind him, citing apparent evidence of nights out that they had taken with friends, it was all petty and circumstantial, but what broke him was that his health was being used against him. His health had been failing.

The month before he received the news he had spent his life dreading. His kidneys were failing. His kidney function had dropped to below 30%, stage 4... Though he knew stage 5 wasn't far off.

They had sat together listening as the doctor talked about the next steps, looking ahead to the possibility of dialysis and kidney transplant. The disease had also impacted other organs causing a cyst to develop on his liver which was the cause of his recent discomfort and back pain.

That appointment would have sent him spiralling, but with Frankie even that news wasn't enough to break him. They could beat anything together.

"What's the timeframe?" Frankie asked.

Rob was too numb to ask questions.

"That is like asking how long is a piece of string..." the Dr replied.

"But... If I was a betting man I'd say at most we were a couple of years away if the decrease in GFR continues at the rate it has been..." the Dr continued.

Rob sat in silence holding on tightly to Frankie's hand.

"The best thing you can do is start to make plans, maybe start looking at possible donors, family members.

They returned home, both in shock.

"Right" Frankie declared determined to get ahead of the situation.

"First. I'll get tested... I know it is a longshot, but it is worth trying... You never know we could be a match" Frankie continued trying to be hopeful.

"And….. We're going to see your mother"

His mother appeared apathetic to his situation as though the news was nothing. Rob mentioned the cyst on his liver, to his astonishment she rebuked him claiming that was due to his drinking and lifestyle rather than his kidneys.

"Are you willing to be tested?" Rob asked.

His mother claimed she was too old, and maybe she was. Owen was the first to voice his stance as he stood in the doorway listening to the conversation. They contacted Gregg and Isabella, they also refused to be tested.

That month had been like a rollercoaster. The refusal to even be tested was like a kick in the gut, like kicking him when he was down. He was devastated. He couldn't understand why.

He knew they hadn't always seen eye to eye and his relationship with his brothers at times was strained but he always thought blood meant something. To him it was as though they were wishing him dead. He knew that had they ever needed anything he wouldn't have turned his back even after all they had done. Another blow arrived in the form of Frankie's results; she wasn't a match though he knew she would have given in a heartbeat if she had of been. That was the only thing keeping him going, her constant love and support giving him strength. She wasn't ready to give up, he knew he had to keep going for her and Katrina.

The letter he was holding in his hand mentioned his failing kidneys but also his 'liver disease' used as more evidence to back up his apparent addiction. That broke him as he knew Raquel could only have gotten that information from his mother. Out of all the betrayals, all the times she took the side of others that one cut deepest, almost deep enough to kill him.

For a few days all he could do was cry as he was broken. Frankie watched not knowing what to do or say, her anger building as she watched the love of her life in so much pain and heartbreak. He was so selfless and caring yet they made him out to be a monster, he couldn't understand what he had done for them to hate him so much. He was growing weary of it all and had enough.

A week past with Rob feeling as though he should accept defeat. He was growing weary, he'd had enough, he couldn't take anymore. He'd lost his daughter for good.

Still though he needed answers and had just a small amount of fight left within him. They sat in the car outside his mother's house watching as Raquel picked up Katrina. They seemed like a perfect happy family.

He was filled with rage. He walked up the path braying upon the door, his key no longer worked, the locks had been changed, he guessed to keep him out.

Owen answered the door. Rob stood in front of his mother's home being restrained by his brother.

Rob walked away realising that it was over, to him they were no longer family. The games they had played had taken a toxic turn. They had gone too far, past the point of no return. He knew it was time to cut all ties.

Father's Day was fast approaching. His first Father's Day without his daughter, that day it hurt the most not being able to see her, all he saw were some pictures posted on Facebook, as though put there to taunt him.

Mid-day on Father's day his phone pinged, a message from Greg, a photo of him holding Katrina and the words Happy Father's Day.

It felt as though they were all taunting him, Frankie felt sick to her stomach.

Frankie watched as though life was draining from him, like he was dying slowly in front of her. His eyes were so different, the light and love had faded, they appeared grey and almost jaundiced. The man she knew had gone and she didn't know whether she could bring him back, and if he would ever be the same again.

The days that followed were some of his darkest days, days where he didn't know whether he could keep going. He kept being drawn to the kitchen, to the wine rack which housed various bottles of alcohol. He kept picking up bottles, holding them in his hands and staring as though trying to fight the urge to drink away the pain. Every time he resisted. The promise he made to himself on her birthday all those years ago and his love for her was enough for him to resist. He also knew that doing so would prove them all right, that it was the reaction they were expecting.

All she could do was love him and hope her love was enough. Days past.

"We're ok, you and me?" Frankie asked as he walked around as though a zombie.

He nodded as though it took every ounce of strength. Her hand cupped his chin, he stared into her loving eyes knowing that she was the medication he needed to survive.

The following weeks Frankie comforted him as the depths of the deceit became more apparent, made worse by the constant barrage of nasty and sometimes sick messages from Raquel. It was the hardest thing he ever had to do but they decided to cut all ties, to stop fighting. Rob consoled himself with the thought that it wasn't forever, that one day sometime in the future he would be able to again have a relationship with his daughter.

They may have lost the battle but not the war, that one day when he was stronger, they could fight back. He took the decision to change his telephone number, and to delete and block his family from all social media.

Those following months felt like a weight had been lifted. They could no longer get to him; it was just the two of them. Rob grew stronger. Frankie could see remnants of the man she fell in love returning, and without the interference it felt like heaven. She felt full of hope.

She concentrated on creating memories.

Chapter 19

August.

Rob sauntered around the kitchen. The hours when Frankie was at work always dragged.

His phone pinged to indicate a message had been received. He turned over his phone which was lying on the work surface. To his astonishment it was a message from Imogen. He stared at his phone in disbelief, wondering what the message contained. His mind ran through many scenarios. It had been years since they had spoke, not since that fight back when he was trying to work and save for his wedding.

Occasionally he had thought of her, sometimes triggered by songs or events.

He took a deep breath and clicked on the message.

Hi stranger (and you're stranger than most..)

That line made him smile remembering when he wrote those same words to her a lifetime ago. He re-read that line a few times and every time he read it his smile grew bigger. He continued reading the remainder of the message.

You probably don't want to talk to me... Who could blame you, I am a shit friend, that is if I am even deserving of that title? Maybe I lost that privilege a long time ago.

He pondered... Had too much water passed under the bridge to salvage anything from their friendship?

I Hope you are well. God that sounds so casual!

I've been thinking of you a lot the past couple of years. I have a picture of us at prom, and picture of me you and Marcus from my wedding beside my bed.

You know I kept all your letters and sometimes I find I need to read those wise words spoken to a hopeless pathetic broken girl. Reading them brings back so many memories of our time together. I always knew I was wrong; I was a selfish cow whose only defence was that she was scared of losing her anchor.

You were a huge part of my life, you saved my life, and my happiest memories from college and Uni all involve you. We had some good times, didn't we? I haven't been well, I got a bit of a scare, you know they say your life flashes before your eyes, well I found myself worrying that I might not ever get the chance to let you know how much I love you, and how much I valued your friendship and have the chance to apologize for the many times I was a crap friend.

Hindsight and age has made me realise how I wasn't always the best in return..... I really miss you.

Do you ever think of Scarborough?? Ok I'm changing the topic....

I visited not long ago, catching up with Simon and Gary and many others, the thing is you were missing.

I don't know, maybe there is too much water under the bridge for us to ever be friends again, but I just want to know that you're doing ok, that you're happy. That your life has turned out how you imagined it. Please just let me know you have received this. Even if just to say there is no hope. So I can at least know you have received my apology. Ok it's all me again... Sorry.. I have changed honest!

I hope life has given you everything you ever wanted.

With all my love

Imogen x

A smile crept upon his face as happy memories flooded back.

"Alexa play Sophie B Hawkins.." he shouted into the living room.

He sat contemplating his reply. What had she meant by 'she had been ill'.

He wanted so badly to reply, to ask what was wrong, to fall back into that role of being her rescuer, her saviour, her friend...

But her betrayal had cut deeper than even the most recent of betrayals.

He typed a reply.

Hi stranger. Have missed you. Am OK x

Though he knew he wasn't OK but it felt as though he needed to reply in platitudes, still keeping that distance as though to protect himself.

The dots began to move along the screen as though to indicate that Imogen was writing a response.

I am so happy that you have replied... You have made my year! I kept wanting to message you over these years but thought you would never reply, I guess not knowing was better than the realisation that we were done forever, that my behaviour was past the point of no return... But hey there is me going on about me, me, me again.

So sorry... Let's start again... How are you really? Are those kidneys behaving? How is Buzby? How is your mum? How is Frankie? I saw your wedding pics.. They are awesome. Though you have put on weight. Guess she's feeding you well!

He thought about the question 'how is your mum?' Imogen had always known that the relationship with his mother was at times balancing on a knife edge, but he knew she could never have envisioned his reality, even he never imagined he would end up where he was.

He replied keeping it short.

We are all goooood x
So what's this about you being ill??

A few minutes past. He sat listening to music, randomly asking his Alexa to play old songs which had been on their playlist, each song brought back a flood of memories. Frankie had bought him it as a Christmas present. When he first opened it he thought it was a bit naff, but soon he realised it was the best gift she could have given him.

His phone pinged..

We're not talking about me.. This isn't going to become a pitty party, I didn't get in touch so that you can rescue me once more. I can stand on my own two feet, I'm a big girl now…. She says……

Imogen had taken her time in writing her reply. She was determined to be strong, not to break down for him to swoop in and save her. It would have been all too easy to write all of her problems in the hope his selfless caring heart would heal her.

She wasn't going to allow that, wanting to start on a fresh footing, that she would be there for him, that she would spend a lifetime making up to him for her behaviour, and to find a way to repay the debt that she owed, the debt of friendship. The wall she had built would take a long time to break down, first she felt she had to earn back his friendship. She also thought how he had declined to open up about his health, she always worried, always wondered would he reach out if needed?

She continued to type...

What have you been up to?

Rob sat thinking. He asked himself how could he reply?

I haven't been up to much. How about you? How is Marcus? I like your profile picture. It's nice.

A friend request popped up on his phone. He accepted and began scrolling through her profile, photos, and newsfeed as he awaited her reply.

Imogen slowly typed her reply. Her world wasn't all roses, but she had to make out her life was at least ok.

Been working hard. I need workaholics anonymous!! You know me lol. Been working on a few gigs, got on the telly! I finally made the big time…. Well OK, I wouldn't say big time, just backing dancing, blink and you miss me… but it's a start right? Marcus is his usual self, working himself into the ground.. So really nothing has changed..

The room fell quiet. Rob looked up from his phone.

"Alexa play Paula Cole"

Very busy indeed… Wow. Sounds like a hoot, and looks like one too from your pictures. I'm still listening to sixpence non the richer and capercaillie you introduced me too. Listening to Paula Cole, where have all the cowboys gone. Oh and Buzby is in the garage, is SORN. Maybe one day we can get her back on the road though I don't know if I can ride her, doubt she'd hold my weight, cause as you pointed out I've got a bit chubby! Whatever has been wrong?? I hope you get well soon. Thinking of you x

Imogen sent a reply

Thanks. We really do need a catch up sometime. Maybe we can pop up soon? Hate that we've drifted apart so much. You were always a massive part of my life and even if you never realized it you were what got me through a lot of really tough times, not counting the number of times you saved my life.

She meant those words, though knew visiting was going to be hard. She didn't want him seeing her like that, and her and Marcus had been struggling to adjust. Also, to hear him so proud of her. It was better to keep up the pretence. She hadn't lied, she'd just been economical with the truth. The reality was nowhere near the dream she had spent a lifetime trying to achieve.

Hey, signing off for tonight but you don't give yourself enough credit. I didn't save you. You saved yourself... I just walked... OK Rode with you through some of the journey.

Imogen read those words over and over wondering if he had lived the same reality as she had. She thought how the greatest virtue in God's eyes is humility, and he had that in abundance, a lot more than she ever had. He was always selfless whereas too many times she found herself to be selfish.

She began to cry. Her tears were a mix of tears of happiness at being given the grace to be allowed to again be his friend though she didn't feel worthy, but also tears of regret and guilt feeling as though she had failed, kicking herself for leaving it so long, longing to be able to reverse time to be able to make up for the time lost.

Rob sat in reflection at the conversation allowing himself to feel happiness, without her in his life it always felt like there was a small piece missing. He looked up at the clock, his smile grew as he realised that Frankie would soon be home, the days always dragged alone without her.

"Right!" he exclaimed as he stood up to make sure the house was tidy and dinner would be ready for when she walked through the front door into his arms.

He took being a house husband to another level. He could no longer work, he couldn't provide so this was the way he contributed. It wasn't simply about creating the sort of space she deserved, but also it helped create the ability to take control of his life with a steady consistency, to become reliable and good enough for her.

Even after all those years he still never felt good enough.

Frankie returned home from work and instantly noticed that something had changed within him. Over those months, although there had been some normality, and some great times, there was always still an element of darkness as though there was always a dark cloud following him. Sometimes he managed to escape it, to outrun it, but it always managed to catch up to him. That evening she could see a spark, glimpses of the man she fell in love with.

"You seem a bit chipper today?" Frankie casually commented as they set the table for dinner.

"Oh, yeah forgot to say Imi messaged today"

"Oh" Frankie uttered in reply, not knowing what to reply, or what she felt about it.

She had picked up the pieces when their friendship ended, just like she had to pick up the pieces whenever anyone tried to break him.

Rob sensed her reservations.

"It's OK... She apologised, we talked. It's going to a long road to get back to anywhere near what we had but it feels good.."

Frankie listened; her mind awash with possible replies. She looked at him with those eyes of love.

She was willing to watch and wait. She hoped that rekindled friendship would help him, she'd heard so many stories over the years, but deep down there was a small hint of jealousy, she had been his world, she was his protector, his hero, it had become the two of them against the world. She formulated her reply..

"Well that's good.. you were good friends and I guess you should never lose sight of that... I just don't want you to get hurt anymore... From anyone..."

The following day as Rob sat staring at the four walls he continued to allow wild memories to flood his mind.

He picked up his phone.

Morning Imi.. Hope you're doing fine and dandy. Friday the 13th! Ahhh! HaHaHa! Think I'm going to go tinker with the old girl. I mean Buzby.... I remember how your mind works!

"Right!" Rob declared standing up, walking towards the garage.

Over those coming weeks and months they began talking more, finding their way slowly back to some remnants of the friendship they once had. Both still remaining guarded, both believing they had forever.

Over those months Frankie began to drop her guard, gradually getting to know Imogen over Facebook and videocalls, a friendship of their own was slowly beginning to blossom. So many times they all talked of plans, plans to meet up, adventures they would take together but always life got in the way.

Chapter 20

Christmas was quickly approaching, the new year on the horizon. The renewed friendship had in turn sparked a determination for Rob to get back on a bike. He knew it wouldn't be easy but knew it would be worth it, that even the discomfort and possible pain would be worth it. Frankie had told him she would pay for one, he just had to choose one. Frankie listened as he excitedly flitted from one bike to another. He would choose a bike being resolute that it was the bike he wanted, for then to do a backflip and throw another bike into the mix.

She began planning for his birthday that following February to surprise him with a bike, the problem was she knew nothing of bikes. Frankie picked up her phone sending a text.

You busy?? If not call me x

A few moments passed. Her phone rang indicating a video call, she pressed accept.

"Hey! What's up?" Imogen asked seeming out of breath, sweating..

"Have I caught you at a bad time? You can call later..." Frankie replied looking at the screen watching Imogen as she walked, dressed in gym gear.

"Nah, its fine. Friends come first and I've got a break in rehearsals... So... What's up?"

Frankie told her how she had agreed to buy Rob a new bike and spoke of her frustration that every time she thought he had decided on a bike, and she had made enquiries to get that bike, he would change his mind.

Imogen couldn't help but laugh.

"Sorry I know I shouldn't laugh, but I thought you would know that is like putting a child in a sweetshop and asking him to pick just one" she replied through her laughter.

"So how can I help?" She continued while trying to restrain her laughing.

"I know shit about bikes!" Frankie replied.

"I thought maybe you could help? I'm planning on getting him a bike for his birthday, I just need someone who knows bikes, and knows Rob to help... So, I thought instantly of you." She continued hoping Imogen would help.

"Yeah sounds good... How's about end of January I come up for a couple of days, I'm sure in that time we can sneak in a trip to the showrooms on Scotty Rd and buy something"

"You sure?" Frankie asked.

"Yeah, anything for you guys, and any excuse to look at bikes, wish I could get another myself... Window shopping is the perfect antidote" Imogen replied feeling happy that she had been asked, feeling happy that although it was taking a long time, her friendship with Rob was being fixed, and also a new friendship was being forged.

The guilt she had carried with her was beginning to subside, she felt as though she was beginning to atone for her mistakes, the forgiveness enough to control the regrets from continuing to eat away at her. She was looking forward to the future and allowing herself again to dream.

Christmas.

They had decided that Christmas would be a Christmas like no other, Frankie's mother and brother were joining them for the celebrations, to make it a perfect family Christmas.

Frankie went all out, the biggest tree, the most extravagant decorations, and hanging Christmas stockings from the fireplace.

That Christmas Eve, although tinged with the knowledge he wouldn't see his daughter, he felt so very blessed.

Rob was the happiest that Frankie had seen him since losing his family.

That year he was more thankful for his health, which he knew some wouldn't understand. He was feeling well, in fact better than he had in a long time, he was grateful for the present, and energised with the happiness that filled his home.

He was grateful for all of the love and support his wife had provided, not just that past year which but their whole relationship. Through sicknesses and family betrayal she supported him. She was the centre of his universe, his guiding light in the darkness. He planned on spending the rest of his life devoted to her, never taking her love for granted. She was 1 in a million, no.... 1 in a billion...

He opened the final window of the advent calendar to find the image of an embrace, of peace and good will. As he stood there, he thanked God for her, and for the gift of spending his life with her.

Rob and Frankie sat huddled together by the lights of the Christmas tree on the settee like they had so many nights in their many years together. The Christmas carols played in the background adding to the ambience.

Christmas day was the embodiment of the celebrations, a feast with the table adorned with candles and crackers. As Frankie and her mother moved within the kitchen creating the final touches, they could hear Rob and Brendan laughing. It sounded refreshing to have the house full of laughter again, it was magical.

That day they all ate too much and drank too much. Frankie's mother commented on how it truly was the best Christmas ever. Frankie resolved to make every Christmas like that, with each getting better and better.

What she didn't know was that our paths sometimes take unexpected turns, and that Christmas was to be their last.

Chapter 21

Mid-January.

Rob's birthday was on the horizon, Frankie was excited to put her plan in action, she just had to wait for Imogen to arrive. A week before she was due to arrive Frankie received a phone call.

"I can't make it, I'm really sorry, hate letting you down, I've failed again, I'd move mountains to be there but am stuck in jail yet again" Imogen spoke sounding deflated.

"Jail?" Frankie asked, a little puzzled but also disappointed.

"Hospital, but it may as well be jail... just don't let Rob know" Imogen insisted.

"But..." Frankie started.

"Please.. I know I don't deserve to ask that of you..." her words trailed off... pausing creating a silence which could be cut with a knife.

"I've got an idea!" Imogen spoke excitedly breaking the silence.

"Late birthday/early Anniversary present….. I can get you tickets for the Gold Cup in September, and if I come up mid-august, we can get a bike and surprise him with both… That way you also get a weekend away in Scarborough??"

"Sounds good but I'm not camping!"

"OK, deal" Imogen laughed. She hadn't laughed for a few weeks, at the point of feeling like giving up, but making plans gave her the strength to keep going.

"Look after yourself… I'll check in soon" Frankie replied.

The call ended. She didn't feel comfortable keeping that declaration from Rob but guessed she had her reasons, though she knew one of those reasons was guilt and making an over exaggerated effort to be selfless, as though to fall on her sword, a way to earn the forgiveness she already had.

Frankie sat thinking, looking for a plan B. Her mind filled with ideas of how to celebrate and what to give him. She was going to make it a day to remember, wanting everything to be bigger, better, a way to make up for all the loss.

His birthday arrived; the sun was shining brightly in the clear blue sky. The day was quiet, just the two of them. It was the perfect birthday in every sense, and in all the ways only the universe can give.

Spring had come early, the first spring blossom opening on the trees as though especially for him. An unexpected letter from a friend, as a reminder of times gone by and a rekindled future.

They celebrated with an afternoon tea, plenty of cake and wine. The cake was chocolate upon chocolate. The centre was rich and sweet, the coating was double cream mixed with melted chocolate. They began by eating a slice, but all to soon Rob became mischievous like a child high on sugar.

He scooped some cake in his hand chasing Frankie around the garden. He got great pleasure in catching her and smothering her face in chocolate before licking the remainder off his fingers. He then looked at her with those puppy dog eyes as she tried to feign being mad, but she could never be mad at him, that cheeky grin which always followed was enough to make a smile begin to creep across her lips which enveloped into a laugh.

He then stepped in closer, his hand softly touching her face before wrapping his arms around her. She let her head rest upon his chest for a few moments. All her thoughts stopped as they always did when she was safe in his arms, as though secure in a serenity where their souls could dwell forever.

As always, he began gently squeezing her as if he needed to check she was really there with him, really there and really real... Frankie doubted if anyone else ever felt the way she did in his arms, the kind of love that spans far longer than one lifetime.

They spent the afternoon sat in the garden basking in the sunshine, drinking. He enjoyed the day with an inner glow, the kind that showed in his eyes.

Frankie had bought a large foil helium balloon for Rob. The balloon which was attached to the garden table was beginning to move in the delicate afternoon breeze. They sat drinking while watching the clouds pass-by, giggling searching for shapes within the clouds.

Rob's eyes were drawn to the balloon, his sneaky cheeky grin began to again creep across his face.

"Shall I let it go and see how far it gets." He asked like a giddy child trying not to laugh.

"Yes yes" She said as though baiting him to let go.

He looked at her as he unfastened the gold ribbon, holding it in his hand, before slowly opening his hand to allow the ribbon to glide up his palm, carried by the force of the helium.

They laughed as they watched the balloon carried on the breeze.

"What if it hits a plane?" he said, regretting what he had done.

She could see the scenarios playing in his mind.

"It won't get that high" she laughed but it did go very high.

That caring selfless heart was what she loved most, his kindness, his compassion where there was also grace, his integrity, and that smile. Her hand touched her face transferring a small remnant of the chocolate from earlier onto her finger,

"and his sense of humour!" she thought to herself laughing as she watched him staring into the sky.

"Another glass?" Frankie asked breaking his attention.

She picked up her phone taking a picture of him, a picture to capture that memory forever, he pulled a face in return, she couldn't resist taking another, to capture that side of him.

They sat in the garden till well into the evening, as the sun began to set, and the garden became lighted by the solar lights which draped along the wooden fence. They laughed so much that day, it was amazing, though little did she know it would be his last birthday.

It was happiest she'd ever seen him. Just the two of them together, inseparable.

Chapter 22

August.

Frankie lay awake in the early hours, early Sunday morning... The plan to purchase a bike was in full swing, Imogen was due to arrive in 2 weeks, the tickets for the Gold Cup booked, all that was left was to pay for the hotel, and of course buy the bike! Frankie looked over at Rob lying next to her, it had been a while since he had moved, lost in a deep sleep.

She lay there watching him, while her sleepy eyes scrutinized the contour of his face, soaking in the fine details that mapped out his cheekbones and jawline. A view she could never get enough of, he was so handsome as he slept, that steady heart, those steady breaths, more than enough to make her fall in love with him all over again.

As she lay resting her head upon his bicep her body fused with the curve of his body, while her other arm draped over his slender abdomen. It was as though gravity tethered her to him, her body sinking deeper into him, so close that the warmth between them blended. His body provided a sense of security, joy, excitement, and peace. There was never anywhere else she wanted to be, she relished every dying second, lying there next to him.

For some reason she began to reminisce remembering the moment his beautiful face entered her view and her life. She had never met him before but from that moment she was smitten, all that consumed her mind from that moment was him, he became her everything.

She thought back to that first morning waking up with him beside her, watching him sleep, something she wanted to continue for the rest of her life. It was, however, the most ordinary moment in the world, but a moment she could never forget. There were no facades, no preconceptions, and no expectations.

From that day life simply never stayed the same; it moved with a love that was all encompassing, something which she knew she had never experienced in her life, and something she knew he had also not experienced. She thought how they had lived more in those few years than many could ever live in a hundred lifetimes.

The darkness in the room began receding, replaced by a creeping faint blue and orange light. The dawn was breaking. She didn't want to move; she wanted that moment to last forever as though something was telling her to cherish that feeling. She buried her face into the side of his neck and closed her eyes.

Little did she know that their time wasn't infinite, but in short supply, not knowing that beautiful and perfect morning waking in his arms would be their last.

Not knowing that she would never again awaken to the sight of seeing his face or would ever hear his voice again. That she would forever crave his return, the ache for one more morning.

Those few days before felt different. Rob was filled with a sense of neediness, needing to be near her, holding her, wanting her by his side, repeatedly telling her that he loved her, never wanting to let go, as though somewhere deep down his senses were foreseeing the coming future.

The Tuesday before that morning he was with her brother. They had spent the day looking after his Aunty following her return home from a by-pass operation. His Aunty and Uncle were the only family he still had, family who loved him. Frankie had watched as he doted on her.

───────────◆◆◆◆───────────

Frankie returned home but Rob decided to stay a bit longer to make sure she was OK. Brett also agreed to stay, to help but also for the company.

As she sat at home her phone seemed to ping incessantly with messages of how much he loved her. There was a short lull in messages before again her phone began to vibrate. She picked up her phone with a slight annoyance but when she looked it wasn't a message but a phone call from her brother.

She answered and in that moment her heart stopped, her phone fell from her hand crashing to the floor. Rob had collapsed and was unconscious. Frankie ran out of the house into her car desperate to get to him. When she arrived, he was on the floor but was beginning to gain consciousness again. He sat up confused unable to remember what had happened.

Brett stood in shock wondering whether to ring for an ambulance.

"Hey mate.. No…. I'm OK" Rob insisted as Frankie sat holding him.

After a short while Rob began to feel almost normal, he insisted he would be OK, that he would see his GP. They returned home and went to bed. Rob lay awake asking her to stay awake with him.

They lay together. Rob watched as she fell asleep in his arms, he watched her sleep, not wanting to close his eyes, deep in his mind he worried that if he did, he may never wake, and never see her again.

Instead of sleeping he lay awake reminiscing. Remembering how they became inseparable from the beginning. He thought how it felt as though they were one from that day on.

He looked at her with his tired eyes thinking how he was as much in love with her that day as he ever was, perhaps even more so. He thought how if death was on the horizon, he was content. Though he would fight to stay by her side, he wouldn't go easily as heaven had nothing on being with her.

He awoke the next morning, and the next few days were as normal, as though the events of that Tuesday were forgotten as Rob continued to care for his Aunty, running around after everyone else, the GP appointment slipped his mind. Though no matter how much he tried to escape it, the sense of something not being right hovered like a dark cloud, like an elephant in the room.

Frankie slipped out of his arms trying not to wake him, quietly walking out of the room and downstairs into the kitchen to make his morning coffee. She stared at the present which lay upon the dining room table, a pink box wrapped in white satin ribbon.

They were going to a friend's christening that day. She returned to the bedroom as he began to stir, smiling at the sight of his beautiful wife.

As she placed his coffee upon his bedside table his arm encompassed her pulling her into him, pulling her back upon the bed in an embrace leaving her with a lingering kiss.

"Come on, we don't have time... We've got to get ready" She replied pulling away slightly before leaning back in for one final kiss.

His penultimate day upon the earth began as a day of happiness, a day celebrating a new life, and a time to celebrate being alive, to celebrate being with friends.

The air tasted so heavenly as they walked to the small chapel, the short service followed by a party to celebrate at the local club. They ate, and drank and danced, but mainly spent the time sitting watching friends.

The day was filled with smiles and laughter, filled with love, but as the sun began to set it wasn't only the darkness of night which ensued.

As dusk began to set, Rob began to notice his lip was beginning to swell, he became nauseous as though struggling to stay in the present, having moments where it felt as though he was watching himself, and watching everyone.

He tried to laugh it off not wanting to ruin the day for his friends, thinking he could deal with it later, it wasn't important, it wasn't serious...

They returned home. Frankie looked at him and could see fear in his eyes.

11.45pm. Sunday night.

The nearest hospital had recently been downgraded from an A&E to a walk-in centre, the nearest A&E was over 30 minutes' drive. Rob continued to say that he would be fine, a mix of not wanting to worry her, to not be an inconvenience knowing she had to be up for work the next morning, but also out of fear.

Frankie refused to take no for an answer, watching his face slowly begin to swell and seeing the colour gradually fade. She drove up to the nearby hospital to find the door closed with a sign indicating patients to go to Cramlington.

She looked over her shoulder at Rob sitting in the passenger seat. She clambered out of the driver's seat, her legs like jelly. Her hand fell upon the bonnet to support her.

She took a final glance at Rob giving her enough strength to find her balance and began running towards the glass doors.

She began to bang on the doors screaming for someone to help as pain throbbed through her body, feeling as though someone had their hand in there squeezing her organs removing every ounce of life, she could see him slipping away and with him slipping away it was as though she was also dying, as though his life provided a lifeline to hers, and with that line becoming severed she was becoming starved of oxygen.

A nurse approached the glass door.

"You have to go to Cramlington" she spoke calmly.

"He won't make it!" Frankie cried as she fell to her knees.

The nurse opened the door, looking over at the car she pressed an alarm.

As Frankie remained glued to the floor her mind flashed back over the past week, that Tuesday, and that day, asking herself why she hadn't done more, hadn't insisted he get seen sooner.

They rushed him past her with no-one paying her any attention.

Rob began to lose consciousness, the pain that once burned like fire began to fade away to an icy numbness, an empty space filled with a thick static. His heartbeat pounded loudly, echoing in his ears, as he tried to fight against it.

He began fighting with every ounce of strength he could muster but began to feel his strength drain away. His eyesight began to blur, but not because of the tears which were welling up. Everything became fuzzy; black filled the edges of his vision; sounds began to fade until the only thing he could hear was his own heartbeat. His breath became ragged, shallow gasps as he struggled to breathe, his tongue was swelling decreasing the intake of air. It felt as though he was drowning. Seconds passed as he lay there until the darkness fully consumed him.

Frankie had remained on the floor, frozen. She stood up in shock slowly walking back to the car. She climbed into the driver's seat and as though on autopilot and began driving, parking the car in the carpark before walking back, walking back through the glass doors, following the sounds of voices and commotion.

What she saw next would haunt her for the rest of her life. She watched as he lay upon a bed in cardiac arrest, his body convulsing as they tried to resuscitate him.

A nurse tried to drag her away as she was overcome and was lost in an involuntary sob.

She screamed for answers.

The nurse stood in front of Frankie with her hands resting upon her shoulders as though to keep her from running to Rob's side.

"His tongue is blocking his airway; you can't be here" she insisted continuing to ease her backwards.

Frankie began to rock back and forth overcome with waves of fear which increased until it was as though she was shaking, her stomach churned causing her to vomit. Her eyes burned with an ache as she continued to sob, as though she had cried for an eternity.

Time slowed and it felt like a lifetime for the paramedics to arrive, taking over, to try and save his life. She watched as his life lay in their hands.

30 minutes passed.

Frankie continued to stand outside trying to look in through the frosted window desperate. A nurse exited the room, the door closed behind him.

"I think you need to say goodbye..." the nurse spoke softly.

"No!" Frankie screamed hysterically as she pushed through the doors running over to the bed where he lay.

The paramedics stepped back looking at the clock. She looked down at Rob looking battered and bruised, the life draining from his body. She wasn't ready to say goodbye.

"I love you.." she whispered kissing him, before looking at the paramedics with a look of desperation,

"Please!" she begged as she fell backwards.

Rob began to hear voices. Frankie's voice. He knew he had to fight, he had to find a way back to her.

"OK!" one of the paramedics declared rolling up his sleeves as a nurse guided her away taking her to the relative's room.

A shock pulsated through his body jolting him back, through the dark he began to see some light, a hazy grey, through his blurred vision he could see people swarming all over him, he realized they were trying to save him.

He could hear a voice arguing with the man who stood over him, saying that it was far too late for him to be saved, but the man refused to give in, and Rob also refused to give in, he wasn't dying, he wasn't leaving everyone he loved behind.

Another 10 minutes past.

A Dr entered the room where Frankie sat waiting. He looked pensive as he told her they had got him back but he'd been gone too long, urging her not to get her hopes up, but she knew he would fight for her, he would come back to her. No matter what he said she was overjoyed and filled with hope.

They transported him into an ambulance to take him to Cramlington. Frankie tried to fight to go with him as she was held back. She watched the doors close and the ambulance pull away, the blue lights turning on.

A paramedic car pulled up in the drop off zone. They urged her in closing the door behind her. Soon she was following behind the ambulance, at times overtaking going faster.

She looked over her shoulder confused.

"Why are they going slower!" she shouted again becoming hysterical.

"It's him who needs to get to the hospital first, not me" she continued.

They arrived at the hospital placing her in a grey room, the clock ticked slowly but loudly. As the time passed the initial shock began to wear off, but as it ebbed away it brought the realisation that she nearly lost him, that she could still lose him, wondering how she could live a life without him.

Frankie's head was pounding. She bent over sharply as though she had been punched in the stomach, bile began to rise up into her throat as though choking her, it mixed with the saliva and splattered over her lap and knees, and onto the floor.

She ran to the sink coughing. She stood there staring at the drain as by slow, torturous degrees, the coughs eased in intensity and then slowly, slowly passed. as severe shock began to set in.

Chapter 23

The hours past as staff came in and out, no-one giving a definitive answer to any of her questions.

A new day was beginning.

She began to stir to the steady patter of rain upon the windowpane, droplets which were catching the emerging rays of the rising sun. The sound bringing a calmness to her mind, a soothing melody, a natural lullaby. She sat up as her mind re-adjusted to her surroundings.

For a moment she could believe it was all a dream, that she was at home in their bed together, living happily for those blessed moments of unity or togetherness. In her mind's eye she was lying next to him. All to soon reality dawned upon her. As she sat up, she rolled her shoulders feeling a knot in her neck from the position she had found herself in. She rubbed the sleep from her eyes, the reality came back into focus, the shock hit her again as her senses tried to make sense of all that had happened.

She couldn't remember falling asleep, she had no recollection of how long she'd been there, with no idea what was happening. If he was OK. She stood up frantically pacing the floor. She needed answers, she needed to reach him.

She remembered a nurse talking about critical care.

She walked through the corridors in a daze scanning the signs, lost, feeling as though she was negotiating through a maze, at times it felt as though the walls were moving, making her feel dizzy. She gripped the metal railing which ran along the middle of the wall. Gripping it she used it to edge forward as though she was climbing uphill. As she turned the corner a sign caught her attention.

Critical care.

She approached the reception.

"My husband...... Robert Reagan" She spoke through bated breath struggling to formulate the words.

A nurse guided her in through the doors, passing her a disposable apron and a mask. She followed the nurse down the corridor which felt as though it was never-ending.

"We had to sedate him to make him comfortable..." the nurse stated as she was guided into a room.

In the centre stood a nurse's station surrounded by individual bays as though standing on a clock face. The nurse continued to urge her forward to a bay. She walked in seeing him lying there surrounded by tubes, wires and machines, the endless bleeping. He looked so peaceful.

She sat by his bed holding his hand. He just looked as though he was asleep, the way he looked most mornings when she would wake up first and just watch him sleep. Nurses walked in an out frequently checking monitors with very few words spoken.

An hour past, a nurse walked in hovering at the end of the bed looking at her.

"He's stable... I think you should go home, get some rest, get some belongings and come back this afternoon..." The nurse spoke with a sincerity, but it still felt as though she was being made to feel unwelcome, that she was in the way.

Part of her didn't want to leave incase he got worse while she was away, and that she wouldn't be there to fight for him. She thought back to the night before when they were ready to give up on him. The memory flashed vividly through her mind.

It was never said directly but she got the feeling that they had given up on him. She'd heard staff say he'd been without oxygen for at least 50 minutes and to prepare for the worst, but she knew he fought to get back to her and he wasn't giving up, neither was she.

"I won't leave him!" she replied defiantly, but in the end they wore her down.

She called a taxi to take her back to Rake Lane to pick up her car.

She stood near the entrance of the hospital watching as the taxi pulled away. The hospital and the car park were busy as people entered and exited the walk-in centre and entered the main entrance for outpatients' appointments.

There was no evidence, nothing left as a reminder of the night before. She became lost in the multitude of sounds, lost in the realisation that nobody knew that her world had fallen apart, did anyone care?

The world just continued as normal, though her world would never be normal again. To her it seemed as though the world was different, as though there was a crack in the fragment of time itself. Birds were flying slower; sounds became amplified while also seeming as though they'd been manipulated. Even the trees had a strange appearance. She stood there as though frozen as the shock began to replace the numbness.

Slowly she began to walk towards her car. There was then a point where everything stopped, the wind, the scent of the flowers, even the traffic, yet she kept on walking.

She sat in her car holding onto the wheel as though frozen. She looked down catching a glimpse of his phone lying on the floor in front of the passenger seat.

Seeing his phone made her think how she needed to tell people though had no idea what to say. She returned home packing a bag.

She lay down upon the bed with her arm outstretched touching his pillow, again remembering the morning before wishing she could relive that moment, to hold it with her forever.

She kept telling herself he would be OK, he would be home soon, but deep down she knew that wasn't true.

Her hands enveloped his pillow. Closing her eyes, she could smell his sweet scent, every part of him ravished her imagination, she found herself ascending into a world of dreams and fantasies as her mind continued to convey the thoughts which were filling her mind and body. She began deconstructing him, as though being back in those early days falling in love with him all over again, back when she discovered new qualities about him that she had never known the day before.

What filled her mind the most was envisioning the way he laughed, the way he smirked, his smile and how time never stopped his smile from melting her heart. Her mind reconstructed memories reminding her of the way she would rest her head upon his lap as he stroked her hair. Moments which were normal and unremarkable but now meant so much more as she realised how much she had taken for granted thinking that those moments would repeat forever. She remembered the way he looked into her eyes, those caring eyes portraying a look of pure unconditional love. Her mind drifted remembering the moments he cried as she held him, remembering the way others broke him.

She remembered how clingy he had been that past week, and the signs which were ignored and dismissed, she wished she had taken notice, sought help, the guilt began eating away at her though knowing it's easier with hindsight to analyse the events.

She fell into a deep sleep.

Chapter 24

"At this time... I'm sorry to say, there is nothing more we can do" were the words of Dr.

Those words hit her as though they were bullets piercing her heart. Her body jarred with each word, the pain seared through her skin and took away every feeling of safety she ever had. She thought how once you've felt love like that, like what they shared you can never imagine a life without it. Her legs began to give way, unable to continue to carry her. How could she go on without him, how could she even live or breathe without him?.

She thought how she never got to say goodbye, she hoped that he heard her words, that he knew she was always by his side. She thought that if he did and was still there then his life was worth fighting for.

Rob lay there, for a moment his eyes opened his vision a blur, it didn't feel like reality but rather being within a dream. He tried to move but was frozen to the spot, that next moment he was standing looking down on himself, tubes covering his body and face. The love of his life there beside him. For her he would do anything to fight his way back, to do anything to survive, their love strong enough to even fight death. The coldness of the air slowly became more apparent, stealing the warmth from the room.

She looked at him. He opened his eyes. A tear fell from his eye, rolling down his cheek.

"He's crying! He's still with us! He's still breathing! How can you say there is nothing more you can do!" she screamed as she found her way back to her feet clutching his hand.

The Dr looked at her desperate state.

"It is just pressure behind the eyes. Maybe it is time to contact people to say goodbye" he answered coldly.

Rob could just about make sense of the words spoken; words jumbled as though listening to sounds underwater. He wanted to be saved, a hand to tow him back to life, to his love, to his world. Slowly it began to feel like that sensation when you're holding your breath under water, the mind fighting for the body to gasp for breath. Slowly the darkness again overcome him, nothing but blackness, a void.

She wanted to fight but it felt as though her whole world was crashing around her; without him she didn't have the strength. The hours passed slowly. That night she cried incessantly. When she thought she had cried every tear she could another flood followed.

She screamed.

"Why us! No!"

She wanted to wake up from the nightmare. She begged God to let her wake up and she would never take what they had for granted ever again.

She remembered the last time he held her. The last time he smiled. She thought how if she knew it would be the last time, she would have never let go, she would have gave her life to save him.

Her emotions ebbed from grief to anger then back again. She wanted answers, she wanted to know why. Her mind kept replaying those scenes like a recurring nightmare. She demanded answers and refused to give in.

Eventually a Dr agreed to speak with her, to go through everything. In that conversation, and conversations following, it became evident that if he'd had a tracheotomy early on, he would have survived, but the nurses at Rake Lane weren't trained for such a procedure. It became apparent that had it not been a weekend there would have been a Dr on-site but as the hospital was downgraded Dr's weren't there on a weekend.

In the end his life was lost due to a moneysaving initiative, he was just another victim of the system. Another blow was the fact that the paramedic had also not been trained for that procedure.

In the end it felt as though it came down to the luck of the draw. The many 'what-ifs' just made her feel even worse.

She fell asleep by his bedside refusing to leave his side. She was awoken early the following morning. She didn't want that day to begin.

An off-hand comment by a nurse made her have the realisation that she needed to let people know. She had entered the small bay in her dark blue uniform, solemn, a serious expression as though devoid of emotion which was maybe part of a defence mechanism working on a ward where most don't leave alive..

The nurse stood at the small wash basin washing her hands as though lost in thought, she portrayed a pensive look as she coated her hands with sanitiser before checking his vitals. Holding the clipboard in her hands she turned towards Frankie, her face softened as she introduced herself.

Frankie stared into space as the nurse continued talking, it sounded like an inaudible noise, but one sentence caught Frankie, as though jolting her back into reality.

"You've done everything you could to save him, you're not letting him down, it really is time to say goodbye."

She found the courage to ring her family, her friends Catrina and Demi. They all dropped everything to be there for her. She knew she had to let his family know, Katrina had to have a chance to say goodbye to her father, though she assumed they would claim she was too young or it wasn't appropriate. She dreaded the call.

His mother seemed so cold, a reply of,

"OK, thank you for letting me know..."

Frankie gave the benefit of the doubt, perhaps she was in shock.

She left a message for Gregg telling him how Rob was in hospital on life support and to ring her, a call that never came. She wasn't going to ring him back.

Her mind began to replay conversations. She wondered whether she had done the right thing in contacting them. Rob had specifically said he didn't want them at his funeral because of how they had treated him, and her, and how they conspired with Raquel to use Katrina against him. She made the decision to let them know as she thought it was the right thing to do, even though it had been 14 months since he'd last seen them. They had pretty much disowned him, and she had to watch how much that broke him.

"Maybe I've made a huge mistake!" she whispered under her breath, while wondering whether he would forgive her.

A few hours passed. She held her phone in her hand scanning her contacts. She knew there was one other person she had to tell, someone who she knew loved her husband almost as much as she did, though really no-one could ever love him the way she did.

Imogen...

She flicked through their messages. Reading the messages made Frankie think of all the plans she had made, the bike. She had imagined the look on his face when he saw his new bike sat upon their drive, that scenario opened the door on all the plans they had made for the future. Thinking of all the plans that were now not going to happen, their life together cruelly snatched away.

Frankie paced the corridor as though unconsciously delaying making the call. She looked at the clock thinking it could be too early, though she knew there was never going to be a right time. She sat in the hospital corridor with her phone in her hand, wondering how she was going to make the call. Carefully she dialled the number taking deep breaths as the ringing tone could be heard. The call went to voicemail.

"Please call me when you get a moment..." Frankie spoke calmly.

A few moments passed, Frankie's phone began ringing, she looked at the caller ID.. Imogen.

She answered taking a deep breath.

"Hey Frankie, what's up" Imogen spoke into the silence...

Frankie remained silent, unable to speak. Imogen's voice sounded happy, she wondered how she could deliver the news that would also shatter her world, just like it had hers.

"Frankie... You there?" Imogen asked.

"Yeah, I'm here...." Frankie answered with a pause.

"Rob collapsed the other night... They had to resuscitate him for over an hour.... They tried to drag me away... They rushed him to Crammy...."

Imogen could hear the panic and desperation in her voice.

"He's a fighter, he'll be OK" Imogen answered, partly trying to convince herself but also to attempt to comfort Frankie.

"No, you don't understand, you're not getting it... They brought him back, he kept fighting but.... " Frankie fell silent as she struggled to say the words out loud.

"....He's in critical care, and they're saying he was without oxygen for too long" Frankie choked through her tears.

All that Frankie could hear was Imogen's laboured breathing as the words began to sink in.

"They believe he's brain dead. But I swear I saw him cry, he's still there... but...." The hope in her voice was failing.

"Look.... They've done tests, all of which have apparently confirmed their original thoughts... They're saying there was no hope, and to contact people to say goodbye...."

"I know you were so dear to him... Do you want to come and say goodbye? I understand if you can't or you think it'll be too hard...."

"Erm yep, of course...." Imogen spoke through broken words, before falling silent.

Frankie continued to listen attentively. The silence was broken by a crashing sound before the phone call abruptly ended.

Imogen's phone had crashed to the floor, falling from her hand as the realisation hit. It was as if her heart had suddenly stopped beating. Her skin went pale as all the colour drained from her. The exhaustion combined with shock made her feel as though she was sinking into a black hole, she felt herself falling. Nausea crept up from her abdomen to her head. The world went black.

A few moments passed. Frankie waited in case Imogen rang back.

Before returning onto the ward, she sent a text.

Please let me know you are ok

Imogen lay upon the cold wooden floor staring at the broken screen, her fingers hovering.

"What do you write in response?" She asked herself.

Everything she typed felt wrong, cold.

I'm OK xx

Imogen typed, hesitating for a moment before pressing send.

She knew she wasn't Ok, she wondered whether she would ever be OK again.

The message flashed up on Frankie's phone, but she knew that like her Imogen would be far from OK. She'd heard the many stories and knew how close they were, or had been, though knowing a bond like that didn't just vanish, and those past few months getting to know her had wiped away any doubts she once had when Imogen got back in touch.

A couple of hours passed with Frankie sat by Robs bed, holding his hand begging for a response, for him to wake up and prove the Dr's wrong.

She walked down the corridor to grab a drink as the Dr's performed yet more tests. As she left the ward her signal returned causing her phone to vibrate in her pocket.

She looked at the phone, opening a message from Imogen.

I'm on my way

As she stared at the message her phone rang…. Gregg.

She contemplated leaving it to go to voicemail... It had been over 6 hours since she rang him.

She answered.

He was very clinical in his tone, wanting to know the facts, what the Dr's had said, never once asking how she was. The call ended abruptly, she had no idea if they were coming or not.

She turned heading back to the ward, back to Rob.

Frankie was informed that the transplant team would be coming to see her. It just made it all feel so final. She thought how they just wanted to get the machines turned off to save someone else, as though his life didn't matter. Part of her wanted to refuse, to say they weren't allowed to turn off the life support, she would stand in their way and fight if necessary. But she knew deep down that there was no going back, and she knew he would want to save someone else, all the way through his life he always went above and beyond to save others.

She remembered Imogen telling her of how he saved her life while risking his. How her stories and the examples of many others over the years were testaments to the fact that when your world exploded, he was the man you wanted next to you. She thought of the many others he'd helped along the way. How he never thought twice about helping anyone yet always brushed any recognition off as though it was something anyone would do.

Whatever he had to do would disappear at a drop of a hat as he refocussed on what needed to be done. There was never a friend in need with him around, he'd stay right there until you could breathe again, walk again... Then he would stand back and let you get back on with your life, never mentioning your crisis again, yet always there ready to pick you up again. His shoulder always available for crying on when you couldn't stand alone.

She thought how he never really said, NO to anything, as though it was not in his dictionary. She thought how he never really said yes either. It was always a "maybe" with a cheeky grin, a grin which everyone knew was really a yes, he always came through... There was always that warm possibility, something loving, inviting., whatever he was asked to do, he did it.

She remembered earlier that year meeting a young man, a refugee who had nothing and no-one. Rob was the only one to show true compassion.

She remembered Luthando thanking him, telling him how wonderful he was, how he was a saint. She remembered Rob's reply...

"Nah mate.... You honestly don't know me yet" he spoke almost laughing.

When the organ transplant team arrived and asked if she would consider giving his organs, she knew what to say.

"Yes.. It is what he'd want" she answered trying to choke back the tears as her friend demi cradled her.

Chapter 25

Imogen sat in the carpark, her hands tightly gripping the steering wheel trying to find the strength to leave the car, to enter the hospital. She felt exhausted from the drive.

She had imagined that drive, that first meeting to be happier, the plans to secretly purchase his dream bike. She wished she had managed to get up sooner, to get up for his birthday as they first had agreed. Her fingers ungripped the wheel before she raised her hands as the grief and regret began to consume her, she'd failed him again. Her hands pounded against the wheel as she screamed, though instead of hitting the car what she really wanted was to hit herself, to punish herself.

After a few minutes she managed to compose herself, she wasn't going to fail him or Frankie now. She tried to have faith, to have hope but she was almost running on empty. She wanted to believe that was still going ahead, that she could break out of that twisted reality she now found herself in. Until she entered the hospital and could see him for herself, she was still clinging on to hope that it was a mistake, a dream, or that a miracle had happened, and he was OK.

That final thought gave her the strength to go in, maybe in the time taken for the long journey North, things could have changed.

Doctors sometimes get it wrong, right? People come out of coma's all the time.

Though deep down as she walked the lonely grey corridors towards critical care, she knew she was fooling herself. The floor was slate grey and the walls an off-white. That hospital didn't exist when she was last there in Newcastle, it looked new, pristine, as though it had never been used. Although she thought how all hospitals lack colour, she thought how this hospital was not like any she'd been to before, and she'd been to quite a few over the past few years.

Hospitals always sent her spiralling, the many hospital admissions had all merged into one, becoming traumatic. The colour and smell made her feel sick and claustrophobic, so much so her body screamed at her to run, to get out.

Her knuckles were whitened and her face paled as she stood, clenching her fist trying to regulate her breathing, just like she had learned following many panic attacks over the years. She looked up. Above, the ceiling was constructed of polystyrene squares laid on a grid-like frame. Imogen counted them as she walked to steady herself.

She entered the critical care ward, taking a deep breath while fastening the disposable gown which she thought had no real purpose. She entered the ward, a nurse's station stood in the centre, and around it was individual bays, like a compass.

As Imogen scanned the room her eyes fell upon the silhouette of a woman, long wavy blonde hair standing over a bed. Imogen had never officially met Frankie, something which she could never understand why, or why it had to take his death to bring them into the same room.

They had talked online and exchanged messages so were not strangers. She began walking closer and closer till her eyes fell upon him, lying there, as though asleep. Her hand reached up resting upon Frankie's shoulder, not being able to find any words.

Frankie turned, embracing Imogen, a simple gesture, saying more than words could portray.

After a few moments Imogen pulled away, avoiding eye contact, looking at Rob lying in the bed. She asked if there had been any change, still clinging onto hope, which diminished as Frankie updated her on the past few hours, telling her how the doctors had begun talking about switching off the life support, something she couldn't bare herself to agree too.

"Look, I've got to go ring his family again" Frankie exclaimed.

Though Imogen could tell in her voice it was not something she wanted to do.

Imogen knew that the relationship with his family had been rocky, it never was perfect, and she'd picked up that over the years that the relationship had become more strained but listening to Frankie's voice Imogen sensed there was so much she didn't know, which just reminded her how much of a failure of a friend she had become.

"I'll leave you two alone while I go ring, and then maybe we can grab a coffee?" Frankie continued before walking away.

Frankie's words made Imogen feel like kicking herself for thinking of herself and her mistakes when his wife had it a billion times harder.

"I have no right to be here" she whispered as she took his hand, sitting there quietly, closing her eyes, as though in prayer, she'd not prayed for a long time.

She had stopped believing she deserved anyone's love, and had turned away from God, and everyone who loved her.

She thought how some days the guilt inside was too much to bear, and this moment had become the straw that broke her.

"I'm so sorry that I couldn't save you, you know I gladly swap places with you right now.... You spent a lifetime trying to protect me, to save me, for me to throw everything away."

"You'd be so ashamed if you could see the girl I've become, and how I broke every promise I made" she continued.

She began matching her breaths to the beeping of the machines that surrounded the bed, the only indications of his heartbeat, his existence. She couldn't bring herself to say goodbye.

"I should be stronger because I think that's what you'd want…"

Her voice trailed off as Frankie approached. Imogen turned away slightly to try and wipe away the tears which were beginning to fall.

She couldn't let her emotions show, she didn't deserve the tears and the consolations. She had one job, to support Frankie, as though in some way she could make amends, to be able to be the support he would have wanted her to be, though she thought how he always had more faith and belief in her than she did.

She began to reminisce remembering how there was once a time when she would hang on his every word, but more so how he would listen as though her words were golden, he listened with his heart, not just his ears. Whatever he said in reply showed his attentiveness, a kindness, a concern that was so quick that, for him, it was natural.

This attentiveness had always been a part of who he was, and if she was honest it was one of the many reasons that she loved him. She wanted so much to be like him though she knew she was never going to measure up.

But she was going to try, starting with the present, she was going to give it her all.

"Hey, want to go grab that coffee... The Dr's want to do their thing" Frankie asked looking over her shoulder at the nurse station.

Imogen thought how she was managing to stay so strong. She wondered how she was managing to still be standing let alone showing compassion to her.

"OK" Imogen replied standing up, her hand slowly parting from Rob's.

They sat in the cafe which resembled a school canteen. The glass windows and seats reminded her of those back at college, back when she first met Rob. As Frankie stood buying the drinks Imogen looked across imagining Rob sitting there laughing, daring her, filling her with his endless love.

Frankie placed the drinks on the table disturbing Imogen's thoughts.

"Thanks" she spoke softly as she took hold of her cup.

"So, did you get through to the family? When are they coming? It'll be good to see them again" Imogen continued.

She could almost read the look upon Frankie's face which told of how things had gotten a lot worse than Imogen had realised.

"What's been going on?" Imogen asked as her hand gently reached forward resting upon Frankie's hand.

"I know they can't exactly win family of the year but..." Imogen's words trailed off.

"They are coming to say their Goodbye's and to bring Katrina but I honestly don't know If I want them here, if I can cope with them here..." Frankie answered. Her words trailed off as she wiped a tear from her eye.

That was the first moment Imogen saw her vulnerability, her true self and true brokenness being revealed through the cracks in the wall which she had erected.

"I know they're far from perfect, but it's good you're giving them this... Even if they don't really deserve it" Imogen stated before opening her arms in the offer of a hug.

"You don't know the half of it! It got worse over the years. Making our life difficult, using Katrina as a pawn in their games..."

Frankie paused as the memories filled her mind, remembering the betrayal which broke him.

"... but what hurt the most was last year... Rob went to his usual check-up and his kidneys had gotten worse... . He'd been becoming more unwell, so we knew it wasn't going to be the best news... His kidney function went down to 30%, stage 4..." She paused seeing the shock register on Imogen's face knowing Rob had kept it from her.

"What.." she replied, her voice trailing slowly, like her words were unwilling to take flight. Her eyes wide, looking forward but not really seeing anything.

Imogen stared into space, lost for words. It felt as though time slowed to an almost stop. A silence, where even the ticking clock appeared to have stopped... The only sound was the thoughts which played in her mind. She thought how once upon a time she'd always been told of how his kidneys were doing and she'd always promised to give him a kidney if needed. She wondered why he hadn't reached out to her, but then she'd broken every other promise so maybe he thought she'd break that one too... Memories of those conversations, those promises, those precious moments passed like thousands of camera frames per second shown one at a time, All the while his insides felt as if there was nothing there, empty...

Then all too quickly time started again, as Frankie placed her hand upon hers, jolting her back to the present, breaking the trance.

"He didn't want to tell you as he knew you had enough on, and you guys were just getting back on track..."

Imogen thought how they had reconnected a year earlier. She had been reflecting over her life and relationships and her many mistakes, the biggest throwing away their friendship out of pettiness. She had been determined to fix things, though thought she had forever to right her wrongs. They were making progress but then she ended up in hospital.

She would have given her life for his, she just wished he knew that.

Frankie paused before continuing to talk which broke Imogen's thoughts, returning her to the conversation, listening attentively though still in shock.

"Over the past year since then his health hasn't been brilliant, his blood pressure kept going through the roof, and began suffering from swelling and cysts but he never let anyone see it" Frankie continued.

Imogen thought how she knew that all too well, he always did hide it, and so did she, like two peas in a pod.

She thought back to that January, she'd told Frankie not to tell him she was in hospital, and although she had every intention on not burdening him, it was impossible to hide it from him as they talked on the phone during those weeks. She thought how just like she knew he would, he had offered to visit, there was never any hesitation, and if she had agreed he'd have been there in a heartbeat. But she hadn't wanted the first time that they saw each other after so long to be under those circumstances. He always rescued her, saved her, that time she wanted to be more to him, give more. She believed that accepting his offer would just set them back on that path.... She wished she could go back, and would give anything to see him face to face, to feel his comforting touch...

Imogen looked up, looking at Frankie who continued to talk.

"Knowing that he was getting closer to needing a kidney transplant we told the family, wanting to plan ahead for the inevitable.... His mother said she would have but was too old...we knew she was too old but it felt more like an empty gesture... but the rest of them all refused to be tested...So basically not being willing to give a kidney if needed... " Frankie stated trying to hold back the tears.

"How could someone do that to family? Kind of like saying go ahead and die... I guess they got their wish" Frankie continued trying to compose herself, not wanting to break down.

"They saw how ill he was but still they played their games, and that Raquel!"

Frankie didn't have to finish her sentence; she knew too well what she meant.

"They always took her side even when she was playing games!" Imogen answered in agreement.

"But... The final blow was them passing that information about his health to Raquel, they conspired together... All access was removed, and they enjoyed using it to hurt him" she continued though felt as though she was glossing over the depths they sank too, finding the memories too hard.

"I'll be with you every step of the way..." Imogen stated.

"You know Owen was so cold when I rang to say Rob was in hospital, he actually said 'and'. It was as if he just didn't care."

Imogen could see the anger and hurt in her eyes. Imogen wondered how she was still standing.

She wanted so badly to find the words to take away the pain but nothing she thought was good enough, she knew she was never going to be enough; she didn't even believe she deserved to be there, let alone give support.

"He had more people who loved him and saw his true worth than those who are too blind to see what they lost..." Imogen spoke though thought how it just felt like empty platitudes.

They returned to the bedside. It looked as though he moved his eyelid.

"See, it's happened again... Please tell me you saw that too!"

Imogen nodded also igniting a small spark of hope.

She watched as Frankie confronted the Dr, to be told it was normal before continuing to say there was no hope, he was gone.

Imogen held Frankie's hand in silence wishing she could find the right words, but as usual she was a failure not realising that those small gestures were the only things keeping Frankie going.

"I know you loved him, and I know he loved you, I've heard so many stories..." Frankie spoke as she stroked his face.

"Maybe you can tell me more of them one day..." she continued.

"Yep, definitely..." Imogen responded though part of her wondered if she would be around to tell them.

Their conversation was disturbed by his family entering. The first thing Imogen spotted was the 30th Birthday badge that Isabella was wearing. Imogen wondered if there was some poetic justice in the fact that her brother would be dying on her birthday, maybe that way she could never forget how badly she treated him.

The little girl in her arms also caught her attention. It was Katrina. She couldn't believe how grown-up Katrina was. She thought how the last time she had seen Katrina she was a baby.

Frankie watched the family act as though they cared. Frankie had also spotted the badge and gained a slight satisfaction that Rob would die on her birthday, hoping that way she would never forget.

Imogen feigned pleasantries. She had always had a good relationship with his family, but also knew the hell they had made him endure.

For a moment her guilt allowed her to have some compassion, for in a way she had broken his heart more than they did, she had also let him down, but her compassion was soon abated as she watched Frankie's body language as Gregg tried to take charge, listening to the tone in which he spoke to her, and the family acting as though they had done nothing wrong.

Imogen thought how they could have easily won an Oscar with that performance, and a glance at Frankie gave an indication that she was thinking the same.

Frankie fought for control refusing to allow him to take over.

The nurses looked on as though to silently declare that too many were by the bedside. Frankie observed the silent cues.

"I'll give you some space to say goodbye" Frankie spoke resolutely trying to disguise the contempt she had for them, gripping Imogen's hand.

"I'll come with you.." Imogen responded as her hand gently brushed against his Mother's arm giving a simple smile. His mother had always been so nice to her, but even so she couldn't get past the way she had treated her son.

"I'll be back soon" Imogen feigned a smile as she walked away following Frankie.

They slowly walked away, though stopped at the nurse's station to reiterate that they had no say and that she was next of kin. Frankie worried about leaving Rob with them but knew she couldn't bear to be around them.

"Hey, we're not going far" Imogen spoke as her hands rested gently upon Frankie's upper arms in a gesture of reassurance.

An hour past. They stood outside of the ICU wondering whether to go back in, wondering if they'd had enough time to say their goodbyes and maybe ask for forgiveness.

Imogen watched as Isabella and Owen walked towards the doors with Katrina in Owen's arms. She looked at Isabella who was smiling, she wondered 'how could she smile?'

How could anyone smile when the world was losing a hero. As they walked out Frankie walked in, head down to avoid eye contact.

Imogen followed behind her, following her back to the bay where Rob lay.

Rosa and Greg remained standing by Rob's bedside. The passing minutes were filled with pleasantries and forced acceptance. Frankie told them she wanted to be alone with rob when they turned off the machines, Greg complained as though he had a self-entitled right.

His behaviour made her feel physically sick.

Imogen looked up at the clock realising it was now time to leave, knowing that the machines were due to be turned off an hour later at 5.30pm.

"Well I think it's time for me to go, give you some time alone before…" Imogen couldn't finish her sentence, she looked over at Rosa and Gregg hoping they would pick up on her silent cues.

"We should be going too, Owen and Isabella will be waiting…" Gregg announced, the animosity present in his voice.

Rosa leant in for a hug to which Frankie reciprocated, though from the look on her face Imogen could tell it was one of the hardest things she ever had to do.

They began to walk away. Imogen hesitated, leaning over kissing him upon the forehead.

"Goodbye my friend" she whispered trying to hold back the tears telling herself she could cry as much as she wanted once she was alone.

She stepped back, her hands swinging as though she had no idea where to place them.

"Will you be OK?" she asked Frankie, leaning in for a hug.

"Yes…Go…" Frankie answered as they held each other in an embrace.

"See ya soon" Imogen muttered as she turned wiping her eye.

She began walking away, looking over her shoulder. Frankie had sat down beside the bed, holding his hand, her head bowed down.

She returned her gaze forward and picked up her step to catch up with Rosa and Greg.

They walked through the corridor, Imogen smiled as they talked recalling some of the moments from their wild years, and although it felt nice to reminisce with those who were there over those years it felt like a betrayal.

They parted in the carpark. Imogen leaned in giving Rosa a hug and looked at Katrina the spitting image of her Father. She wondered if she would realise who her Father really was, or whether her innocent mind would be corrupted with lies. Would she know he was a hero, a man who would do anything for anyone, a man with a selfless heart and a big smile, or would they sell him as a drunk, a waste of space, and any of the other rhetoric's that they told themselves to justify their behaviours.

Imogen sauntered over to her car. She sat down in the driver's seat closing the door behind her. Her hands gripped the wheel, her head began banging against the wheel as she screamed, the tears no longer being constrained.

Back in the ICU Frankie stood alone by his side, feeling scared, wishing time would freeze, feeling broken and traumatised. The thought of turning off the life support was unbearable. As the clock ticked closer to the specified time reality started to set in. The reality that this truly was goodbye, she was losing the love of her life in such a traumatic way, it felt as though she was falling apart.

She had told everyone she wanted to say goodbye alone, she didn't want anyone to see her fall apart, she'd remained strong for too long. She knew that those who mattered got to say their goodbyes, and even those who didn't deserve such courtesy.

She had arranged last rites with the hospital chaplain. She sat by Rob's side crying all the way through, praying for a miracle.

Far too soon the Dr's arrived by the bedside.

"It's time" a nurse spoke softly, placing her hand upon Frankie's shoulder.

Frankie tried to compose herself though felt like she was falling apart, heading for a blackhole which was ready to tear her apart.

She was shaking with fear, she didn't want him to suffer.

"He won't suffer, will he?" she asked almost begging.

She held onto his hand as they turned off the machines. She watched in a daze, as he slowly slipped away.

The Dr's left them alone, allowing her time for a final goodbye, though she had no idea how to say goodbye to the man she loved with all of her heart, also she had no idea how after that goodbye would she be able to go on without him. Without her rock, her best friend, the other half which completed her.

"You can go now my darling" she whispered as his fragile human heart beat for the last time.

Imogen was still waiting in the carpark unable to move, watching the minutes which ticked by slowly.

She knew he'd be gone.

She picked up her phone to send Marcus a text.

Just to let you know, Rob is dead.

Imogen looked up at the sky. A rainbow was breaking through the dark clouds. His voice echoed in her head.

"Let's go find the pot of gold at the end of the rainbow!"

It felt bittersweet. Thankful for the memories but those same memories felt like daggers piecing her soul, slowly killing her.

Looking at the sky, Imogen decided to stay in a hotel for the night, it was getting late and she was too tired. She had been up since 5am for dance rehearsal, and even if she was to go, she had no idea where to go, it felt like the fabric of her life had been torn apart.

On the way to the local hotel, she stopped off at the off license, buying a large bottle of vodka.

"Well, I've got to have a drink to celebrate your life" she exclaimed, though she knew that was just an excuse, she wanted to lose herself at the bottom of that bottle, to write herself off so that she could escape feeling anything.

Frankie walked slowly out of the ICU as though on autopilot. As she exited and the door closed behind her she fell to the floor. The tears began to fall like a tsunami had erupted within her. She cried with more violence than any gale. Not to have him right there was a torture to her soul. She didn't break quietly, it was like every atom of her being screamed in unison, traumatized that she should exist without him. When the wracking sobs passed, she cried in such a desolate way that no-one could bare to listen for long.

She remained on that floor for what felt like a lifetime till her brother Brett arrived. Through her tear-filled eyes she saw his hand reaching for her.

That night when she closed her eyes, she wished that she would not awaken, that she could join him. But the morning came.

She found that waking up was the hardest. He was with her in the void between awake and asleep, but also her dreams were better than reality.

The saddest part of it though, was that eventually even the memory of her dreams began to fade, left with the lonely feeling of detachment, left to explore the empty void of her emotions.

That first day without him was as though she was still lost in a state of shock. She refused to grieve for him as that would have meant having to accept that he was really gone. Although she stood there and watched him take his last breath, to watch him die, there was a part of her that held that memory back. A part of her that could never believe he wouldn't come back, that he wouldn't come bouncing around some corner to laugh at her for falling for this elaborate joke.

But all too soon reality set in. She knew he wasn't coming back.

He was gone forever.

The following days and weeks felt like a blur, she walked around in an almost comatose state, though knowing she had one more task. She could give up and die of her broken heart once she had given him the send-off he deserved.

He'd always said no-one would be at his funeral. She was going to make sure he was honoured.

Chapter 26

The day before the Funeral...

Frankie visited him for the last time.

He was there lying in the coffin wearing the suit he wore for their wedding. She looked in the coffin. He looked so handsome and so peaceful as though asleep. A slight smile played on his cold face. She looked in. She wished he would just open his eyes and smile at her like he always did, but she knew that was never going to happen. She leaned in and kissed him, feeling his cold lips upon hers. He looked calm, he looked happy like he did on their wedding day... but that following day was his funeral... The day their happy ever after ended.

That evening she sat making sure that she had everything in place. She dreaded seeing his family and wished she had stopped them from being able to attend.

Those past four weeks since he had died his family had plagued her life. They knew she was grieving but it seemed as though they didn't care. They acted callous. Greg bombarded her with accusations and wanted information about the inquest into his death, letting slip that they were planning on making a case against the hospital.

Frankie bided her time knowing that they wouldn't be able to make a case without her as next of kin and she would fight to prevent it as she knew their motives weren't pure, they just wanted to benefit from his death.

She recalled how they had called in the days following his death and offered to help pay towards the funeral though Frankie knew that it was just empty platitudes and that they had no intention of helping.

They knew he had nothing due to his health, but it always felt as though they valued a person's worth in money, status, career, rather than a person's actions and heart.

Streaming tears cleansed her red cheeks. A few droplets remained, forgetting their way as the path was swept from beneath them, consequently blurring Frankie's vision with waves of sadness. The tear which managed to escape her hand calmly flowed into her mouth, giving a salty taste, as though she could taste her own sorrow.

They failed him in death, just like they did in life. The final betrayal.

The tears which fell because of them were from a bitter unforgiving pain.

She tried to compose herself. She didn't want their final parting to be tainted by them. She wiped her eyes and breathed in deeply.

As she tried to say that final goodbye fresh tears began to fall, tears of love.

She began to walk out. As she reached the door, she glanced back one final time.

Chapter 27

The Day of the Funeral...

Frankie stood in their bedroom, she looked at her weary reflection in the mirror, dressed in black. She could hear his voice echoing in her mind.

She stood in the room almost rooted to the spot, not wanting to walk out the door because the moment she did, the events would fall in motion. She thought if she stayed there then maybe time would freeze and she wouldn't have to say goodbye. She wanted to stay strong for him, to not break down. She thought how tomorrow she could, but that day she had to keep going for him, she had to give him the send-off he deserved.

"Hey we're nearly ready, the cars will be here soon" Her brother pursed as he peered in through the door.

"I just need a few more moments" she replied as she scanned the room.

Her eyes fell upon the framed photograph on the unit beside the window, a photograph from their wedding. That photograph was all it took for the tears to burst Frankie's dam of restraint. She clutched the solid wooden frame tight in her hand, able to see a ghostly reflection of her face in the thin sheen of glass that covered it.

She looked past her own dreary eyes and stared upon his face that had been caught in a moment of perfection. She focused in on his eyes, they were glistening with the twinkle of laughter that she loved... It was the happiest memories that hurt the worst, they were the ones that cut her deepest, as though shining a spotlight, reminding her of what she had lost.

She clutched the frame tight, pressing it hard to her breasts wishing to feel his head resting upon them one last time... She was numb, yet somehow also in agony. She longed to be with him, wanting him back more than she'd ever wanted anything.

"We really do need to go" Brett urged from the doorway breaking her thoughts.

They arrived at the small church hidden in the centre of the cemetery. As she stepped out of the car, she spotted Imogen standing with Marcus. Frankie walked over to embrace her.

Imogen didn't know where she fitted. She wasn't family. She still didn't believe she deserved to be there, or to have Frankie's friendship.

"Come on" Frankie beckoned taking her hand.

To Frankie, Imogen was family, more so than his own flesh and blood. She could see the grief and regrets eating her up from the inside, unaware of the depth of which those regrets had taken her.

Frankie felt as though she wouldn't have been able to get through that past week before the funeral had it not been for her and was blessed by the offer of Imogen making a tribute. Frankie had wanted to speak but the grief was too overwhelming and the thought of his family staring back at her filled her with fear.

Imogen followed behind Frankie. As they neared the old wooden doors of the chapel Imogen spotted Rob's mother…. Standing with her were Jacob's parents!

Imogen stood frozen in shock, numb, catching Frankie off guard. Frankie looked at Imogen, then at Rosa and the strangers who stood with her.

There was a moment before the reality really began to set in, as Imogen's mind tried to make sense of what her eyes were seeing. It was like a camera flash unable to reach the world, stuck in time, catatonic.

"Why were they there?" she asked herself.

"Do you know who they are?" Frankie asked, squeezing Imogen's hand.

Imogen contemplated what to say as it felt as though her brain stuttered for a moment, as though pausing while her thoughts tried to catch up.

She thought that telling the whole story at that time would cause disruption. She wasn't going to allow that on his funeral. She thought how too many times she had been 'the centre', as though everything evolved around her. Reality dawned on her. She needed to protect those she loved, she had to keep moving. He was going to get the send-off he deserved, she could tolerate them for one day. Her hand tightly gripped Marcus' hand as though to give a silent ask for support.

"Erm, they're Jacob's parents... Just leave it for now, I'll tell you all about it later, now is not the time... Don't let them have the satisfaction of ruining today" Imogen spoke in an almost broken voice.

Marcus pulled her in close kissing her forehead.

They walked slowly into the chapel. Imogen was about to take a seat near the back. Frankie took her hand guiding her forward. She sat a row behind, ready to give anything that was needed.

Frankie looked around the crowded little chapel. The chapel was filled with many people who knew and loved him. People who had been able to see and witness their love, the love that had radiated from them, touching the lives of everyone who knew them. She looked up hoping that he was looking down and able to see how much he was loved, how many lives he had touched, and also see the many lives that he had saved just by being there.

Mid-way through the service Imogen stood up and slowly walked down the aisle to the wooden pulpit. She stood there for a moment shuffling her notes.

"I'm standing here to tell you about this amazing man. To tell you about a man who saved a broken girl. I can imagine many of you could stand here and share similar stories. The thing is he never believed that what he gave was special or that he made a difference, I guess that is what made his selfless and humble heart even more special."

Imogen paused. She was resolute to not break down, to not cry. She had to remain strong, she had to grief on the inside, believing that she had to hide her sorrow from everyone. Though no matter how hard she tried it could be seen in her eyes, her movements, her drooping posture.

"But I'm also here to talk on behalf of Frankie... Something which is an honour. Very few get to find what they had...."

She wiped her eye to catch a single tear.

"He once wrote in one of his many letters to never cry at his funeral, and that if I did, he would never speak to me again, so I will try not to cry... He also said death could come to us at any time and that he was regularly putting his life in my hands when he ate my cooking... Well, I must say, my cooking wasn't that bad, but it has improved!"

Her words made her smile and a small giggle played upon her lips as she visualised him roasting her over her disastrous cooking skills. She cleared her throat before continuing.

"They say there is no reason. They say that time will heal... But neither time nor reason will change the way we feel... No-one knows how many times we have broken down and cried. Rob, if you're looking down, I hope you have no more doubts. Because although you're wonderful to think of, you are so incredibly hard to live without.... A thousand words won't bring you back, I know because I've tried... and neither will a thousand tears... I know because we have cried.... We want you to know how much you were loved...." Imogen paused, before continuing...

"Those words are true, but they feel like empty platitudes... So, I'm going to talk about the man I knew.... About the man who saw a scrawny, scared young girl and decided to go out of his way to help her, the man who saved a broken girl from those determined to crush her spirit..."

As she spoke those words she glanced over at Jacob's parents for a fleeting moment. She hoped they realised that comment in part was aimed at them but also their precious son... She refocussed looking up the aisle trying to avoid eye contact with anyone except the odd glance at Frankie and at Marcus when she needed strength to continue.

"The man who wrote letters to her every day, and frequently told her she was someone, she was worthy, she was loved... The man who jumped on his bike at a moment's notice to ride at high speed to stop a girl standing on a cliff top considering stepping off...."

She took a breath trying to compose herself.

"I know that nothing I could ever do could have made up for all he did, nothing I ever did even came close... I have many regrets that I will have to live with, and maybe many of us do... Did we really know what we had?"

She glanced briefly over at his family hoping that they also felt the overwhelming weight of guilt and regret, and that maybe that day would be a turning point and they would begin to try and make amends for all the wrongs they had done. She couldn't read them; She didn't want to believe that there wasn't an ounce of compassion.

"But enough about me....."

She glanced at Katrina sat upon Greg's knee.

"I remember when little Katrina was born and the love that Rob had for that little girl. The way his eyes lit up, the way his world evolved around her, daddy's little Princess... I just hope as she continues to grow that she will know how much he loved her and that he would have moved mountains for her..."

Imogen paused. She was seriously doubting that would be true, that she would know the truth, but instead continue to be fed lies and falsehood. Imogen diverted her gaze to Frankie.

"Then there was Frankie, the one person who never let him down, and the person he loved more than anything. I can't find words because there are no words that could do justice…"

Imogen paused looking back down at her notes.

"But actions are louder than words… Everyone could see the love that Rob had for Frankie…. I remember when he met her. He had always laughed at me and my belief in love at first sight, soul mates and all that soppy stuff, but I was proved right when he fell head over heels in love…. Frankie, I know I never saw him as happy and content as he was with you, and he truly did blossom when he married you…. A love like yours lives on forever, death has no power."

As Imogen glanced down at her notes, she felt as though she had managed to conceal her emotions, but everyone bared witness to her "tears inside" openly displayed within her demeanour. You could read her like a book, as she turned to the last page of her notes.

"I have some words to read from Frankie….. You were my world, my soulmate and my best friend. You touched my life in such a loving and kind way… You swept me off my feet. I will love you forever. Being without you is unbearable but I know you will be with me in my heart for the rest of my life…"

Imogen paused again.

"I know many more who loved him, all of us here did... He was loved by Frankie's family, he was a treasured nephew, and a loyal friend to not just me but many others. I've heard it said you die twice... Once when they bury you, and again when the last person speaks your name... I know I will never stop talking about him, and I know neither will Frankie... As long as we never forget him, he will live with us forever..."

Imogen bowed her head as she walked quietly back to her seat, thinking that nothing she could have ever said would encompass the amazing diamond that had lived among them, a diamond tossed aside by so many who never saw his true worth.

In part she believed he was an angel who had been called back home. His job complete, but that would never be a comfort to Frankie who now had to live without him there, though Imogen knew that even death itself wouldn't keep him from her.

After the service they walked to the grave. Imogen held Frankie as they watched the coffin being lowered into the ground.

"Ashes to ashes... dust to dust..." The minister spoke as he tossed a handful of soil upon the coffin as a symbolic gesture of the burial to come.

Frankie threw a rose, which was then duplicated by Imogen. They stepped back as others proceeded to throw roses upon the coffin. Frankie took one final look before walking away, heading to the wake.

Frankie tried not to allow her focus to fall upon his family, but instead kept busy talking to many guests who retold stories of how her husband had impacted their lives. How much of a pleasure it was to know him, and to be able to count him as a friend. Finding relief in the wild stories, the crazy memories. Each story gave her the strength to keep going. Stories of him dropping off food parcels to those in need even when he had nothing himself, the hours spent helping a friend in need, the biker arriving on the roadside to help a stranded car or bike.

Each story adding to the narrative of her unseen hero. The hero who helped anyone in need. The man who walked into a room and changed the atmosphere, the man who never allowed anyone to be an outsider... Everyone also spoke of how much he had loved Frankie, and how you could see the love between them.

She took a fleeting glance over at his family, at Greg lording it over everyone, Isabella and Owen seeming unphased that their brother had died, and his mother sitting with the uninvited gate-crashers. She knew that Rob would never be accepted by the likes of them, he didn't fit into their 'box'. He stood out, he dared to be different, but in that difference was also a genuine heart. She thought how if you fit in with them you can't stand out, and Rob certainly stood out, and everyone knew it.

At the wake Imogen watched Jacob's parents overloading their plates with food and taking a bottle of wine for themselves. They made small talk with her as though none of their history existed. She stood tall as she told how she was a professional dancer and had performed in the west end and on TV and was married to a fireman.

In a way she wanted to show them they had been wrong about her, though in part she felt like a fraud, her life had not been as rosy as she had made out, but she couldn't allow them the satisfaction.

Imogen however took great satisfaction in dropping in a passing comment to Rosa how the son of her friends hated Rob, and that the feeling was mutual. She smirked as she walked away, back towards Marcus for an embrace, then back to Frankie to make sure she was OK.

All too soon the wake was over, one by one people left. What was a filled concert room soon became empty….

"You know I'm always going to be here, whatever you need, whenever you need…" Imogen gestured to Frankie as she embraced her in a hug.

"I'm not going anywhere… she continued as they hugged, glancing over at Marcus who could read the deeper meaning behind the comment.

"We're moving back up to Scarborough, hoping to get a house on the Mount... So, I won't be too far away... You never know... I might get back on the bike so I can get here and back faster"

Imogen laughed winking.

"Buzby will need someone..." Frankie replied as she remembered the many hours he had spent trying to fix her to get her back on the road.

Remembering him walking back into the house covered in oil and smelling of petrol. Remembering the smell of petrol mixing with the smell of his body odour and his favourite deodorant, thinking how at times the smell was overbearing but how now she would give anything to be held again in his arms with that scent lingering, encompassing her.

Imogen smiled as memories of Buzby filled her mind, thinking how it would be a great honour to one day ride her again.

They parted. Though Imogen couldn't bear to see Frankie return home alone...

Chapter 28

Frankie returned home. The knowledge that life would go on without him, that time was only stopped for her, undid her completely. All pretence of quiet coping was lost. She had remained strong for so long. The funeral had kept her going but now that was over there was nothing to live for.

She collapsed upon their bed no longer caring if she lived or died, though dying felt like the better option, that way they could be reunited. Those following hours and following days were the darkest, at times wanting to just fall asleep and never wake, to die to be reunited with her love. She truly felt as though she was dying of a broken heart. She couldn't find any purpose to life, constantly asking why.

His bible lay open upon the windowsill where he had left it. Staring at it she screamed at God for taking him from her so soon.

His death had been so sudden, so brutal. She knew his health was bad and that they may not have managed to grow old and grey together, but she thought they would have a lot more time and more time to come to terms with the idea of death, many more years to make memories.

Every morning she woke up, and for a moment she forgot, in that moment between awake and asleep where he was still there. Every day was like losing him all over again and every day she died inside.

She also never got answers... The funeral had been delayed due to the autopsy but that had never brought an explanation to why his tongue had swelled. There was no closure.

As the grief continued to overwhelm her, she continued to slip downwards which led to her losing her job which made living harder, she just wanted the world to swallow her.

Two months after the funeral Frankie was sat in her living room feeling lost, a glass in her hand, the alcohol numbing some of the pain, without it the pain was too real. The phone rang...

"Hello..." Frankie said as she answered the call.

"Where is the headstone?" came the reply...

Frankie was thrown by the lack of compassion.

There was no 'how are you? Are you coping?'

Instead, just cold accusations.

She resisted asking where the money they had offered had gone, instead she stood in shock before allowing the phone to fall to the floor.

She had spent every last penny of her savings to buy the headstone... A headstone with his photo and a beach scene which was an almost replica of the beach in Jamaica where they had married...

The day that her and Rob were happiest, she had wanted the stone to be the perfect tribute to him....

It just wasn't ready yet.

In a way that cold call was needed... It jolted her back into reality.

Rob had always said no-one would visit his grave after he was gone, that he would be forgotten. They had talked of death on many occasions, maybe because he was always aware of it. She remembered those conversations. How so sure he was that no-one would visit his grave, that it was selfish for him to expect anyone too.

Frankie always responded with the same response.

"I will always come till the end of my life, your grave will be full of flowers, always"

She knew that if she died, that what he believed would likely come true... The only other person who visited the grave was Imogen sporadically when she was visiting.

Frankie decided in that moment that she would honour that promise, to visit the grave every day till she breathed her last breath, and that it would forever be adorned by flowers.

Chapter 29

Imogen sat at her desk scanning the photos which surrounded her, pictures of her and Marcus, pictures of her with Frankie. Her eyes fell upon a photo... The photo of her and Rob at prom.

It was a year to the day that he died. 365 days without him yet the world seemed to continue.

She thought how they say you die twice, the first when you take your final breath, but also the last time that somebody mentions your name. She thought how it was also said that a person never leaves you as long as you carry them in your heart....

She'd heard those quotes so many times and had reeled them off her tongue many times to comfort grieving friends. Though, until the day he died those words were really just empty platitudes which now felt all too real... You see, now somebody close to her had died.

Someone she owed her life to...

"Rob... I'll always remember us this way" she whispered as her finger brushed against the image of his smiling face.

The day he died 12 months earlier she had made a mental note, a sacred promise to mention his name at least once every day in some desperate hope that this would keep his memory alive, to keep him close, but it hurt. Every time she spoke his name it hurt, the regrets, the grief...

She closed her eyes each time his name left her lips and after some months, it didn't hurt as much anymore, instead it brought comfort...

She stared down at her computer screen; her eyes drawn to the blinking cursor upon a page of the office document.... A manuscript.

She had been writing his story, wanting the world to know about the hero who saved her, knowing she owed her life to him.

Her phone vibrated on the desk beside her. She picked up the phone to reveal a message.

Be arriving at the Grande in 20! Got balloons and plenty of Gin!

Imogen smiled sending a quick reply.

See you soon!

She took a deep breath in, holding it for a moment before exhaling slowly. She clicked save before closing the document, and the computer. Glancing back up at the photos she smiled.

The only good thing to come out of the loss of an angel was the friendship which had slowly grown over that year between her and Frankie, two women united in their love of one man. What started as just trying to make amends and keep a promise, as though to make up for all the broken promises, became a real friendship. To Imogen that friendship and forgiveness helped to heal the wounds from the guilt and regrets which had almost broken her.

She stood for a moment as her hand hovered above the light switch.

"You always led me astray in all the best ways...and now your wife has taken the baton" she laughed as she turned off the light walking out and closing the door of her study behind her.

She walked casually down the stairs, her hand gliding along the white banister. Her bags stood against the front door ready.

As she stepped out of the house the sun was almost blinding, the perfect day for a ride, the perfect day for racing, the perfect day to celebrate a life.

She passed Buzby who sat in her garage.

"We'll be out for a ride soon girl!" she spoke as she gently stroked the blue tank, before walking to the small car which sat adjacent.

The anniversary of his death coincided with the Gold Cup; it had been moved to a couple weeks earlier as though by fate. Frankie was joining Imogen in Scarborough with them staying in the Grande for the weekend to remember him in the way he would have wanted to be remembered, a weekend of fast bikes and alcohol within the safety of the town which had become his refuge for so many years, a place that had stayed with him.

It felt poetic to attend the event together to honour him, though in an ideal world they would rewind time and be there the previous year as planned, she knew it would never be the same without him.

Imogen placed her bags in the boot, climbing into the driver's seat she declared...

"Let's do this!"

She arrived at the Grande, awaiting the arrival of the coach.

She watched as Frankie stepped off the coach and fell into an embrace.

"Let's go have some fun!" Imogen exclaimed.

The Saturday they spent in the town, down the amusements, and karaoke in the packet... Imogen shed a tear as she stood on the small stage singing bat out of hell. Memories filled her mind remembering the many days and nights there. She closed her eyes; she began to sing.

As she opened them it was as though she could see him standing there, leaning against the wall like he had so many times before with that smile that said...

"You go girl!"

It felt as though he was there with them, she just had to close her eyes to feel his presence, to hear his laughter.

They met up for a drink with Gary revisiting stories of a time gone by.

After, the girls walked along the esplanade almost drunk as they recalled stories of Rob. They laughed and cried, like they always did. It was as though they had both found someone who understood.

A year had past so people expected Frankie to be over the grieving, or at least for it to not be so present, she sensed many were beginning to tire of hearing the stories and she began to feel the need to set limitations.

To everyone else life was continuing...

To Imogen, apart from Marcus it felt like no-one understood. No-one grasped how she could grief a 'friend' to that extent.

But together there was no limits, no need for either to curb their emotions.

That night they partied falling through the hotel room door in the early morning.

The Sunday they spent watching the racing. As twilight began, the Mount again becoming empty, they walked to the memorial to set the balloons off to honour him and remember him.

As they let off the balloons, watching them be caught by the wind and rising as though heading to the heavens above, Frankie thought how she had managed to keep going and to make it to that anniversary. Surviving day by day with the help of good friends and family, and secure in the knowledge that he would forever be with her.

She thought back to a few nights earlier, waking to see him standing beside her.

"I love you…. And God loves you" she heard his voice clearly, a voice she could never forget…

His arms surrounded her filling her with an overwhelming feeling of love and peace. But too soon he was gone, though she knew he would always be there.

She could feel his presence always with her, he had never left her. She knew he would never leave because what they had lived on forever.

He had found love that even loved him at his worst moments and arms to encompass him at his weakest. He had found someone to save him, to give him years of happiness, the type of love he'd never dreamed of or ever believed he deserved.

She had become his light, his soul, his everything.

The End..

Though with love there is no ending.......

Truly.. Love conquers all...

It conquers hate.

It overcomes despair,

and can even conquer death...

About the Author

Alexia Lockhart is a wife and a mother who is also a romantic with a love of reading and writing romance and poetry. Her writings were always kept hidden, a bit like a personal diary.

Only 2 people saw her writings, her best friend who inspired this book, and encouraged her to never give up writing, and her husband who is her strength.

This book which is the first part of a spin-off book was written as a prequel to the Wildflower Series, written to honour her best friend, an incredibly special man, an angel.

 A man who sadly passed before seeing his story.

Other books by this author

In time you will learn more about the two characters Imogen and Marcus. Learning their back stories and what makes them who they are. Some books are still being written, check-out the website for more information.

Nobody's Hero. Part 1.The Wildflower Years.

The prequel to this book following Rob's story, written in real-time, before he met Frankie. Learn about the hero who saved a broken girl as he tried to save himself.

Becoming Wildflower.

The first book in the Wildflower Series. We meet Imogen at the end of her second year at university as she begins to struggle with life. She is encouraged to look back over her life, looking at what made her the young women she was, and those who influenced her Life. In this book we are first introduced to Rob, the friend who saved her. There is a lot of cross-over between this book and nobody's Hero Part 1 as we see their friendship through her eyes.

Wildflower - Becoming His.

The second book in the Wildflower series. In the book Imogen meets Marcus. The book is an erotic romance. There is an edited version, though still has some erotic content.

Wildflower Belonging.

The third book in the Wildflower series.

Look deeper into the aftermath of Rob's death from Imogen's POV and see her look back and take stock of her life so far.

Is there ever such a thing as a fairy-tale happily ever after??

We also follow Imogen and Marcus as they navigate through married life. As they encounter troubles including chronic illness, depression, PTSD, abuse and loss.

Can they find a way to support each other, and be each other's rock?

Difficult roads often lead to beautiful destinations but only if you work at it and never give up.

Wildflower Captured

The fourth book in the series which goes deeper into one part of book 3, another erotic romance which just compliments book 3

Connect with Alexia Lockhart

I really appreciate you reading my book! Here are my social media coordinates:

Find my page on Facebook:
https://www.facebook.com/Imogenkelsie/

Follow me on Twitter:
@imogen_kelsie

Follow me on Instagram
@imogen_kelsiewildflowerseries

Visit my website:
https://www.imogenkelsie-thewildflowerseries.co.uk/